"I'm not totally helpless, you know!"

Mallory went on explaining to Bren. "I've looked after myself for years now . . . and that includes replusing any unwanted male attention!"

He nodded in mocking acknowledgment. "That's heartening news." Without warning he pulled her close, one hand tilting her chin upward. "Perhaps you'd demonstrate if some fellow starts something like this, just how you'd go about it?"

Shaken by her sudden unbelievable awareness of him, Mallory tried to conceal her feelings.

"In this case, there's no need," she claimed. "We both know how you feel about me, so I've no worries."

"Haven't you?" Bren countered, his hands pushing into her hair. "I doubt any man could remain unresponsive to you for long . . . and I guess I'm no exception." Then his mouth closed determinedly over hers. . . ."

Kerry Allyne developed wanderlust after emigrating with her family from England to Australia. A long working holiday enabled her to travel the world before returning to Australia, where she met her engineer husband-to-be. After marriage and the birth of two children, the family headed north to Summerland, a popular surfing resort, where they run a small cattle farm and an electrical-contracting business. Kerry Allyne's travel experience adds much to the novels she spends her days writing—when, that is, she's not doing company accounts or herding cattle!

Books by Kerry Allyne

HARLEQUIN ROMANCE

2479—MIXED FEELINGS
2515—VALLEY OF LAGOONS
2527—SPRING FEVER
2593—SOMEWHERE TO CALL HOME
2647—TIME TO FORGET
2725—MERRINGANNEE BLUFF
2737—RETURN TO WALLABY CREEK
2761—STRANGER IN TOWN
2809—THE TULLAGINDI RODEO
2869—CARPENTARIA MOON
2929—LOSING BATTLE

Don't miss any of our special offers. Write to us at the following address for information on our newest releases.

Harlequin Reader Service
901 Fuhrmann Blvd., P.O. Box 1397, Buffalo, NY 14240
Canadian address: P.O. Box 603,
Fort Erie, Ont. L2A 5X3

Beneath Wimmera Skies

Kerry Allyne

Harlequin Books

TORONTO • NEW YORK • LONDON
AMSTERDAM • PARIS • SYDNEY • HAMBURG
STOCKHOLM • ATHENS • TOKYO • MILAN

Original hardcover edition published in 1988
by Mills & Boon Limited

ISBN 0-373-02947-0
Harlequin Romance first edition December 1988

CHAPTER ONE

MALLORY SCOTT definitely needed a rest. After three years spent modelling in Europe and the United States—during which time she had only been able to manage to make it home for a brief ten-day holiday some eighteen months previously—she had gradually experienced an increasing need for a lengthier break and, on the spur of the moment, had booked her flight to Australia.

Home was a property called Avalon in the Wimmera, a noted wheat and sheep-raising district some two hundred and fifty miles north-west of Melbourne, where her beloved stepfather had always been the manager—initially on behalf of a local grazier, but for the last year for a city-based corporation—and Mallory had been eagerly anticipating the chance to relax in the hot summer air and to re-charge her batteries, so to speak, as she mulled over her future.

What she hadn't expected, however, was the totally dampening news her stepfather imparted at breakfast the morning following her arrival. That he would ever resign from his position as manager of Avalon had just never occurred to her.

'But—but why?' she stammered on finally recovering a little from the shock his disclosure had wrought, but with her lovely, wide-spaced and duskily framed violet eyes still clouded with confusion. 'Don't you like working for the Banfield

Corporation as much as you did for Clyde Gilroy?'

Ward Melrose's lips shaped expressively. 'Well they certainly tend to keep a closer eye on what you're doing, I must admit, but that's not the reason, all the same.' Pausing, he shrugged his broad shoulders and gave a rueful half-smile. 'No, I guess you could say it's more a case of knowing one's limitations.'

Mallory frowned. 'Meaning?'

'Meaning, that where crops are concerned, I've been a wheat-grower all my life, but unfortunately present market trends dictate that particular grain to be about the least desirable to grow,' he elucidated on a wry note. 'In other words, the world is glutted with wheat, and as a result I suspect Banfield's will be wanting diversification—as some are already doing—in the form of other crops; speciality crops geared to different markets, and to be honest . . .' with a sigh '. . . I think I'm too old a dog to be learning new tricks at my age. So I figured it was time to get out and leave the field to someone younger.' He shrugged again.

Never having heard him talk so fatalistically before, Mallory found his words hard to digest. The more so since, at fifty-five and with hardly a day's illness to undermine his health either before or after her mother's untimely death some eight years earlier, he had certainly never seemed old to her.

'But surely, if others have managed to make the change successfully, you could, too!' she put forward urgently. 'Would it really be that much more difficult to grow something else?' A sudden, indignant, suspicion came to mind. 'Or is it Banfield's who are actually giving you the push because *they* have someone younger in mind for the job?' She knew they were a hard-headed coporation with an emphasis on youth.

Ward leant back in his chair, shaking his greying head and smiling a little. 'No, it's nothing like that. It was entirely my own idea. Besides . . .' he hesitated, his gaze not quite meeting hers ' . . . that isn't the only reason.'

Mallory drew an anxious breath. 'Then what is?'

'You remember Cecily Horne . . . ,' he began slowly.

She nodded. Cecily was a widow who lived in Nyandra, the small town nearest the property, and with whom her stepfather had struck up a friendship during the time Mallory had been overseas. He had introduced them the last time she had been home on holiday and she had liked the older woman immediately.

'Well . . . we're thinking of getting married,' Ward disclosed, and his blue eyes sought hers worriedly. 'You don't think I'm being disloyal, do you?'

'Disloyal?' Mallory returned his gaze perplexedly. Then, on abruptly realising, 'Oh you mean, to Mum's memory, and all that?' She shook her head, smiling reassuringly now. 'No, of course I don't think that. How could I when, even though you and I aren't related by blood at all, you were still more than willing to keep me as your daughter even after Mum died?' Reaching across the table, she clasped his hand with long slender fingers. 'No, if you want to marry Cecily, I can assure you that you have my blessings and congratulations, and I hope you'll both be very happy.' A slight pause, and her expression turned quizzical. 'Not that I can quite understand just what bearing your possible marriage has on your resignation, none the less.'

Obviously relieved by her response, Ward relaxed. 'Well, Cecily isn't really interested in leaving town and living out here. After all, she's lived most of her life in Nyandra, and she has her own house——'

'But so do you—here!' Mallory cut in defensively.

'Except that it's really the company's house—not mine—and then only for another five years when I would have to retire and leave, anyway.'

That was a circumstance Mallory hadn't ever considered. 'So you're really just retiring early?' she mused in doleful tones.

'Not entirely. I don't feel I'm quite ready for the scrapheap just yet,' Ward disclaimed with a half-laugh. 'As a matter of fact, I've sounded out a few people in town, and I don't think I'll have much trouble in getting work down at the saleyards, or at the grain-receiving depot.'

'I see,' Mallory acknowledged quietly, nodding. Everything appeared to be settled, and apparently to his satisfaction, at least. Yet she still couldn't help declaring in a partly protesting, partly despondent fashion, 'But I've always thought of Avalon as home! It's always been there in the back of my mind—like a welcoming haven from the rat-race of city life and big business! And—and why didn't you mention what you were considering in any of your letters?' A hint of accusation entered her voice.

Ward eyed her apologetically. 'I intended to once I'd received word back from the company.'

'So they haven't actually accepted your resignation as yet?' Could that signify a chance, perhaps? Not that she supposed they could stop him leaving if that was his intention, she reluctantly had to concede.

'No, they haven't as yet—I only posted it five
days ago—although I see no reason why they
wouldn't. No one's indispensable, or irreplaceable,'
he replied duplicating her own grudging thoughts so
closely that she expelled a heavy sigh.

Now it was her stepfather who clasped her hand
comfortingly, his gaze fond as it took in the beautiful
features that were her greatest asset as a model; the
pure oval outline of her face, the slender nose above
a wide, engaging mouth, the long-lashed amethyst
eyes that normally weren't shadowed as they were
presently, but glowed with vitality and zest for
living; the flawless skin like creamy alabaster, and
the long and blunt-cut ash-blonde hair that reached
past her shoulders like a shimmering, silver silk
curtain.

Tall, at five foot nine she was only a couple of
inches shorter than he was, but whereas he was built
on thick-set lines, she had a perfectly proportioned
figure that was voluptuous and yet still managed to
convey a sense of fragility, and as a result was
guaranteed to arouse emotions of envy in women,
and immediate interest, not to mention
appreciation, in men.

Ward couldn't have loved her or been more proud
of her, and her phenomenal success in her career, if
she had been his natural daughter, and he hated
knowing that it was his actions that were the cause of
her downcast demeanour now.

'I'm sorry, pet, but I just didn't realise the place
had come to mean so much to you,' he said in
contrite accents. 'I mean . . . it's what, four years
now since you left here as an eighteen-year-old to
seek modelling work in Melbourne? And despite

your present unexpected visit—though very
welcome, I can assure you—I'm afraid I just never
imagined that, when you did return to this country
for good, you wouldn't simply take another
apartment in Melbourne, the same as you did when
you first began modelling, and continue your career
here.' His anxious eyes held hers earnestly.
'Although there will always be a home for you—a
welcoming haven—wherever I live. And as Cecily
fully agrees there should be, I might add, so you've
no worries in that regard.'

Mallory did her best to summon up a grateful
smile. 'That's very kind and generous of her, and of
you, too, of course.'

The only trouble was, any such home wouldn't be
at Avalon, and she doubted anything could entirely
compensate for that. It had been her home since she
was eleven, and she really couldn't remember all
that much of her life before then, especially those
even earlier years before her father had died at such
a young age. At least, she couldn't remember much
except that they had been difficult times for her
mother and, in consequence, it had been a case of
their continually moving from one lot of rented
premises to another. So many times, in fact, that she
had lost count.

Then Ward had come along, and with him,
Avalon. Combined with her mother, they were all
she could ever have asked for, and more. It had also
been Ward who steered her so steadily during the
months that followed her mother's death some three
years later. But Avalon had been there again, too,
providing the same security, the serenity, the feeling
of going on for ever, just as it always had. Or until
now, that was!

'God! How can *you* contemplate leaving here so casually?' she suddenly burst out uncontrollably. 'You've lived here for over thirty years!'

'During which time I've also learnt that people are more important than land,' her stepfather declared on a gentle note. Adding in an even softer voice, 'As you may also come to acknowledge one of these days.'

Mallory bit at her lip in remorse, promptly regretting her uncharacteristic outburst. 'Yes, of course people are more important. I'm sorry, Ward, really I am!' Her eyes sought his forgiveness. 'I didn't mean to imply that Cecily . . .' She came to an abrupt halt, deciding it was probably more prudent to leave that aspect alone. 'It's just that it's all come as such a shock, I guess.' She paused as an unpalatable thought presented itself, making her expression turn rueful. 'And if I'm truthful, I suppose I'm being selfish by wanting everything to remain exactly as it has been, just for those times when I choose to return.'

'Thoughtless, maybe, but I doubt selfish,' he amended with an affectionate smile. 'It has never been part of your nature to be that.' He began pouring himself another cup of tea from the pot on the table. 'But regardless, in view of the fact that there's three months' notice to run, you can at least enjoy the place until you feel ready to return overseas.'

Mallory absently half smiled in response, for the present keeping to herself her doubts as to whether she even really wanted to return to modelling at all, let alone overseas. Oh, it had certainly been an exciting, glamorous and incredible three years, she had to admit. What girl wouldn't succumb to the thrill of having her face appear on the covers of such renowned magazines as *Harper's Bazaar* and *Cosmopolitan,* and of being in demand for some of the most coveted television commercials, not to mention travelling to places as diverse as Paris, Stockholm, Trinidad and Mexico, on various assignments.

It had also been unbelievably profitable in financial terms, but at the same time it was an exacting and exhausting environment, and she was beginning to suspect that it wasn't merely a month or more's rest that she was seeking, but a decision as to whether she should retire from modelling altogether. Although just what she would do with her life if she did quit, particularly now that Avalon wasn't to be a part of it, she had no idea. Thoughts of the property recalled her stepfather's last remarks, however, and had her eyeing him curiously.

'Three months' notice, you said? Is it company policy to require that long?' It seemed a somewhat excessive length of time to her, not that she was objecting, of course. The longer the better, as far as she was concerned.

Ward shook his head. 'No, but since there isn't really any great urgency to my leaving, I thought I might as well make it easier all round by giving them plenty of time to find a replacement.'

Mallory nodded, a teasing light entering her eyes. 'So just when are you and Cecily thinking of . . . tying the knot?'

'We—umm—had been considering early autumn,' her stepfather said gruffly, and a trifle self-consciously. 'Or, that was until you arrived home so unexpectedly at this time. Naturally, we would like you to be present, and we had thought that by then you might have been able to take a break, but as it is

I don't suppose you'll be able to get away again so soon, so I guess we may have to postpone it now in order to fit in with your schedule.'

'You'll do no such thing!' Mallory promptly expostulated. 'Good lord, after all you've done for me, do you really think I could condone your timing your wedding for my convenience? No way!' She gave an emphatic shake of her head. 'No, you make your arrangements to suit yourself and Cecily, and no matter where I am or what I'm doing, nothing will stop me from being here, believe me'! Hevens, you mean more to me than any work or schedule!'

Despite being obviously flattered by her response, Ward appeared doubtful. 'You're sure? I mean, I wouldn't want your career to suffer because of me.'

'I'm sure!' she returned decisively. Then, because they had never had any secrets from each other, and it seemed the perfect opportunity, 'In any case, I may not even have a career, as such, *to* suffer by then.' She paused to suck in a deep breath and he waited in watchful silence for her to continue. 'Because I'm not certain I even want to continue modelling.' Her gaze flew to his to gauge his reaction.

Surprise was the immediate emotion that registered on his craggy, bronzed features. 'But you're at the top of your profession, and the last time you were home you couldn't wait to return to it! Moreover, you've certainly not given any hint in your letters that you were anything but extremely satisfied with the way everything was progressing.' He made a confused movement with his head. 'So why the change all of a sudden? Has something happened that you haven't told me about?' His glance became more intent.

Mallory hunched a negligent shoulder. 'Nothing specific, if that's what you mean. More a gradual build-up, I guess you could say. At first I thought it was just a case of having done too much and needing a break for a while, but now I'm not so sure.' Abruptly, she swung out of her chair to stand looking through the window at the sun-drenched wheatfields visible beyond the veranda. 'Oh, Ward, you know what it's like! You avoid going to even Melbourne if you possibly can, and that's nothing compared to some cities! Oh, I know some people thrive on it, but to a girl raised with all this,' waving a hand to indicate the scene outside, 'I'm afraid the endless noise, the crowds, and the pollution, just become too much to take after a time.' She spun back to face him with a graphic look. 'And so, here I am!'

'Implying that it's actually the environment that's making you have second thoughts, and not the work?'

She tilted her head consideringly. 'No, not entirely. I also sometimes find myself becoming a little tired of being told to look—seductive, innocent, carefree, aggressive—on command. Plus, of course, having your face constantly cleaned and made up, cleaned and made up, and your hair pulled into this style or that, also tends to dampen your enthusiasm after a couple of years.' Suddenly, she grinned. 'Both of which are just other reasons why I'm so glad to be here! I can wear my hair how *I* like, for a change, and with no make-up I feel my skin can breathe again at last, too! What's more, I also plan to do the unforgivable . . . and acquire a suntan!'

'Mmm, your skin could certainly do with some colour, you're as pale as a ghost,' Ward commented in matter-of-fact tones, and had her wrinkling her nose at him wryly. 'But why unforgivable?'

'Because a suntan doesn't take make-up well, and that causes problems when you're working under lights.'

'Oh.' His acknowledgement was uttered so vaguely that Mallory couldn't help smiling. Photographic studios, and the techniques involved therein, were so far removed from her stepfather's down-to-earth life-style and work that she didn't doubt that the finer details of her explanation had escaped him. 'Well, if you're wanting to spend some time outside, Dick and I have some mustering to do in the back paddock today, so if you feel like accompanying us . . .' He left the invitation open as he began gaining his feet.

Mallory accepted with alacrity. 'The pair of you won't be able to get out there without me! It will be just like old times again!' she declared with a grin, looking forward to the prospect. Dick Crowley was one of the two hands also permanently employed on the property and she had known him and his wife for many years.

A couple of afternoons later, Mallory was sunning herself lazily on the veranda. By means of judicious exposure, she was delighted to note a faintly golden hue beginning to tint her skin and, propping her long and shapely shorts-clad legs on the surrounding railing, she settled further into her cushioned cane chair contentedly.

This was what she had needed, she mused. Here, she could relax and get her thoughts in perspective; make the decisions necessary for her future. Here, beneath Wimmera skies, where the sun was beating

down satisfyingly from that cloudless track of blue
and where she could breathe deeply of the fresh,
clear air; where the pervading tranquility was
broken only by the sound of leisurely cruising insects
or a gentle breeze rustling the heads of the ripening
wheat; and where the most violent action was likely
to be the lethargic spiralling into the air of a plume of
dust as a vehicle made use of the road that passed the
property.

As if attuned to her thoughts, now there was a
stirring of dust on the road and she watched it
absently, her mind once again making a desultory
effort to concentrate on weighing the pros and cons
of her modelling career. Then, in another moment's
lapse, she suddenly realised that the cloud of dust
wasn't disappearing, but was actually coming
closer, indicating that someone had turned into the
property, and, wondering who it could be, she
waited, albeit still languidly, for its surprisingly slow
approach.

When the vehicle, a Range Rover, did finally
come into view between the golden fields of wheat,
she soon discovered the reason for its delay, for
every few hundred yards the driver would bring the
vehicle to a halt as he apparently surveyed the
surrounding paddocks before moving forwards
again. Probably someone from the Department of
Agriculture, come to discuss and check likely crop
yields, Mallory surmised, and relinquishing her
chair, leant back against one of the roof supports as
she perched herself casually on the wooden veranda
railing and awaited the visitor's arrival.

On coming to a halt in front of the garage, the
man who alighted still didn't immediately make for
the homestead, but stood looking about him

momentarily, and Mallory took the opportunity to scrutinise him—appreciatively, as it turned out.

Being taller than average herself, she immediately approved of his height which was obviously well over six feet. Tall girls liked to feel feminine and delicate, too, and that was extremely hard to do when, especially in high heels, she often found herself looking down on her escorts. That he also had the build to match his height didn't go amiss in her eyes either. Not that he carried any excess weight, that was evident, but his shoulders and chest were the broadest she had seen for a long while, the darkly tanned arms revealed by his short-sleeved shirt hard with prominent muscle—no necessity there for the arms folded across the chest pose adopted by so many male models in order to push otherwise flaccid biceps into shape, she noted—and when taken into account with the long, equally muscular legs moulded to his close-fitting denims, she had no doubts that he was also as strong as a proverbial Mallee bull.

Her overall observations completed, Mallory turned her attention to his face, or at least those features she could distinguish in the shade created by the wide brim of his hat. His age she put in the vicinity of thirty-one, and from the firm, taut lines and planes of his face she surmised those years had been capable and self-reliant ones. What she could see of his hair appeared to be very dark, and when combined with the teak-like toning of his skin, she deduced his eyes would be brown as well. They were too shadowed for her to tell from such a distance. His nose was well shaped, his jaw lean and strong but it was his mouth she found most intriguing. It was at once hard and sensuous, cynical and

generous, and she couldn't help but wonder what
had caused the conflict . . . and which sentiments
prevailed. All in all, she decided, he possessed a
striking face, not a handsome one necessarily, but
undeniably an extraordinarily masculine one that
gave evidence of an assured strength of will and
tenacity within.

When he finally turned for the homestead, he
moved with a loose-limbed confidence and
authority, but as he came to stand on the other side
of the railing Mallory missed his first words, so
engrossed was she with a surprise discovery. Why,
his eyes are blue! she realised abruptly. A clear
cobalt blue, and ringed by thick, sable lashes that
were unbelievably long for a man, so that the
contrast was quite startling. What Duncan—her
previous agent in Melbourne—wouldn't give to
have someone like him on his books! the whimsical
musing followed. He exuded such a virile maleness,
and if he could just be coaxed into smiling a little . . .

'I asked if Ward Melrose was around!' The
brusque statement cut through Mallory's reverie on
a cool and slightly impatient note, and brought a
flush of embrassment to her smooth cheeks.

'Oh, I—I'm sorry,' she stammered, jumping to
her feet, and trying to make amends with an
apologetic smile. Not that she used it deliberately for
that purpose, but normally there wasn't a man
around who could resist smiling back and forgiving
her anything when she looked at him in such a
fashion, only on this occasion it failed completely.
The man facing her remained unmoved. She went
on quickly, 'I'm also sorry to say that, no, Ward
isn't around at the moment, I'm afraid. He went in
for the lamb sales in Nyandra this morning, and I'm

not sure what time he'll be back.' Especially since he had also mentioned visting Cecily afterwards! 'You're from the Department of Agriculture, are you?'

'No.'

'Oh!' Then who was he? A stockman or a station hand looking for work? He dressed like one, and she had certainly never seen him before. Since he hadn't seen fit to expand his reply, she took a chance on her assumption. 'Well, I'm afraid he isn't hiring any staff at the moment either, if that's what you've come about.'

'It's not,' he rejected in deep and strong, but cool, impersonal tones. 'Rather the reverse, in fact.' He paused, eyeing her unwaveringly. 'I'm from the Banfield Corporation.'

Mallory drew a quick breath, suddenly comprehending. 'Oh, you've come about Ward's resignation!'

A sharp nod, and then she abruptly found herself being subjected to a hard-eyed appraisal that surprised her on two counts. First, because it was so far removed from the examinations she was used to receiving from the opposite sex. There was certainly no interest or admiration visible there, she noted wryly. And secondly, because even more unexpectedly, not to say perplexingly, it also seemed to contain a hint of inexplicable contempt.

'You the reason for it?' came the derisive demand at length.

Mallory's eyes widened. Apparently he was unaware that Ward had a stepdaughter, and for some unknown reason seemed therefore immediately to presume that the reason for her presence was a decidedly different relationship between her stepfather and herself! She wasn't sure whether she felt affronted or amused. In the end her sense of humour won out, and she made the decision to allow him to continue in his mistaken assumption a little longer—in retaliation.

'Oh, no, just the opposite,' she replied brightly. 'I adore it at Avalon, and I would much rather he hadn't resigned. But he's such a love, and so good to me, that it's difficult for me to gainsay him anything,' with deliberate, sweetly smiled implication. 'However, I'm forgetting my manners. Do come in, won't you, while you're waiting for Ward, Mr—er . . .?' She gazed at him enquiringly as she swept an inviting hand towards the steps and the front door.

'Dalton—Bren Dalton,' he supplied cursorily, taking up her offer and making for the veranda.

'While I'm Mallory Scott,' she turned to advise over her shoulder, leading the way into the homestead. Then after having shown him to a chair in the pleasantly furnished sitting-room, 'Perhaps you would care for something to drink, Mr Dalton? Tea, coffee, or something colder maybe?' She owed it to Ward to make his employer's representative physically comfortable at least.

'No, tea will be fine, thanks.'

His answer was delivered in the same cool accents as previously, making Mallory ponder as she nodded and turned for the kitchen whether she was doing the right thing in continuing with her little ruse. Still, he had been the one to jump to conclusions, she excused herself as she set about making a pot of tea and preparing a tray, and it would only be until Ward returned, after all, for he was bound to make some remark concerning their true relationship. In the meantime, though, it just might teach the self-possessed Bren Dalton to be a little less hasty with his assumptions in future.

Nevertheless, on her return to the sitting-room Mallory didn't immediately go out of her way to further his belief, but having poured and passed him his tea, sought answers on those matters that concerned her most.

'And—umm—has the company accepted Ward's resignation?' she probed as a result while pouring her own tea.

'I rather think that is no one's business but Ward's and the corporation's.' The snubbing reply was sardonically drawled.

Mallory pressed her lips together. 'Except that, as I also happen to live here . . .'

'Not that you've done so for very long presumably, since you definitely weren't in—er—residence when Banfield's bought the property, nor even as recently as five months ago when I last visited Avalon,' he saw fit to interpose in the same vein.

Only an unaccustomed obstinacy kept Mallory from divulging what could, and perhaps should, have been revealed. Instead, she valiantly forced a dulcet smile on to her lips and countered, 'Although I *am* here now, and in view of the fact that Ward obviously *has* seen fit to discuss the matter in full with me . . .' She eyed him significantly.

'As is his prerogative,' he was prepared to concede, with a slight—she suspected, mocking—tilt of his head. 'Not mine.'

'Oh, for heaven's sake!' she was pushed into flaring. 'I'm not after any world-shattering secrets! I only wanted to know if his resignation had been accepted, or if . . .' She caught herself up, not wanting to jeopardise her own faint hopes by disclosing them in an inappropriate manner, or at an inopportune time.

Bren Dalton wasn't so accommodating, however. 'Or if . . .?' he immediately prompted, his blue eyes narrowing.

Mallory sighed. She was beginning to think she knew, to her cost, just which of those sentiments indicated by his shapely mouth prevailed—the hard and cynical ones! 'Or if . . . you meant perhaps to try to persuade him to withdraw it,' she supplied, reluctantly, but surmising he wouldn't accept any prevarication on the matter now.

For a moment she didn't think he meant to answer, and then he gave an impassive shrug. 'It's not the corporation's policy to do so.'

'And you always follow corporation policy, I suppose.' It was more of an accusation than a question.

Not that he seemed at all disturbed by it as he agreed steadily, 'In the main.'

'Why? Because you don't consider most of your employees worth the effort?'

'Rather because we believe that, unless the position can be radically altered, then it's more than likely the reasons for wishing to resign will remain. And that being the case,' he flexed a broad shoulder once more, 'it's also more than probable that the employee, having once made up his or her mind to the extent of proffering a resignation, will only do so again at some later date, and thus no one's best interests are served.' Pausing he fixed her with a distinctly derisive glance. 'Besides, why all the interest regarding withdrawls of resignations? I thought you said you had no desire to gainsay *any* of Ward's wishes.'

'No, I said I found it *difficult* to gainsay him anything,' Mallory took pleasure in correcting. 'And you might recall I also said that *I* loved it here and that I would much rather he hadn't resigned.'

'Then it would appear you have some differences to resolve between yourselves, wouldn't it, Miss Scott?' he was quick to mock.

Not if he did but know, Mallory mused gloomily, for it seemed he had also inadvertently informed her of what she had least wanted to hear—the corporation intended to accept her stepfather's decision to leave. But at least she was determined to have one success, no matter how irrelevant. That of the joke being on him when he discovered how incorrect he had been about her reason for being there—and to further this end she purposely dipped her head coyly.

'Oh, please, do make it just Mallory,' she invited with a limpid smile that showed her perfect teeth to attractive advantage. 'And I shall call you Bren . . . if you have no objections, of course.' She batted her glossy eye lashes at him outrageously.

'Since I except to be here for some days, it would appear the most logical approach,' he allowed with deceptive idleness as he leant forward to deposit his cup and saucer on the table, and before his own metallic blue eyes shaded with a cynicism that bordered on insolence. 'Provided, that is, you don't anticipate it implying that I'm about to become as tolerant of your unauthorised presence here as Ward apparently is.'

Mallory's initial surprise at learning his visit was to be of some duration was soon replaced by curiosity for the cause of that cynicism. She suspected there was much more to the rugged Bren Dalton than met the eye, and she experienced an overwhelming desire to find out more about him. Meanwhile, however, there was that last remark of his to be dealt with. Unauthorised, indeed!

'Meaning that Banfield's believe they have the right to control their employees' personal lives, too?' she charged in a provoking voice.

'No, just the right to decide how many people shall reside on any one of their properties at any given time!' was the decisive retort. 'So, given that this property has been designated as requiring only a single manager, not a married or otherwise contracted one, *that*, sweetheart,' his endearment was anything but endearingly voiced, 'makes you not only unauthorised, but distinctly unnnecessary and unwanted as well!'

'Except by Ward,' she dared to taunt.

Bren shook his head in determined rebuttal. 'Even by him once I've had a few words to say!'

That was what he thought! 'Although visitors are allowed, aren't they?' she wasn't averse to reminding.

'Not on a permanent basis, no!'

'In that case, since my stepfath . . .' Mallory bit back the rest of the word in horror at her unthinking use of it. One look at Bren's uncompromisingly clenching jaw was more than sufficient notification that her mistake hadn't gone unnoticed.

'Your *what?*' he demanded on a biting note as he pushed out of his chair in one lithe but furious action.

Feeling at too much of a disadvantage while seated, Mallory hastily replaced her cup on the tray, albeit with something of a clatter, and also rose upright, facing him half apprehensively, half contritely. Oh, hell, this wasn't the denouement she had either envisaged or intended! she groaned inwardly.

My—my . . .' was all she managed to stutter in reply before she heard the kitchen flyscreen door bang shut, and she expelled an unbelievably relieved breath to hear Ward's voice.

'I see by the vehicle outside that we have a visitor,' he called out on his way through to the sitting-room.

'Yes,' Mallory confirmed faintly with a diffident look in Bren's direction before all but fleeing to her stepfather's side as he entered the room.

CHAPTER TWO

WITH a smile and a fond press of his hand to Mallory's shoulder, Ward Melrose strode forward to greet the younger man, his hand outstretched.

'Bren! This is an unexpected pleasure! I thought it might have been someone from Banfield's when I saw the vehicle, but I didn't really expect it to be you.'

'It's good to see you, again, too, Ward.' Bren's acknowledgement came in a steady tone as their hands met in a strong grip. Although without any reciprocating smile on his part, Mallory noted in dismay as he continued, 'But apart from the most obvious reason for a visit by a Banfield representative, there are other matters that need to be gone over, including some changes in operation, among other things, that I have in mind for the property and would like to check out.'

Ward nodded. 'Always looking for that extra edge, eh? It's no wonder Joshua Banfield gives you such free rein.' His admiration was evident. 'But it's good if that means your visit will be something more than the flying one you made last time. You'll be here for a day or two, I take it?' He made his liking for the other man's company obvious also.

'At least,' Bren confirmed.

'And you've already met my stepdaughter, Mallory, obviously,' Ward went on in pleased tones, turning to draw that girl forward where she had been standing, discomfitedly, some distance behind him. 'She's been modelling overseas for the last three years—very successfully, too, I might add,' there was pride in his every word, 'and only returned, quite unexpectedly, from America a couple of days ago, so you're very lucky to have actually met her.'

'Very lucky,' Bren repeated with caustic facetiousness—fortunately, lost on Ward—but with such a graphic look on his face when his gaze connected with Mallory's that she reddened and swiftly looked away.

Not for him the discomposure she had anticipated when beginning her deception, nor even now the savage anger that had surfaced when she had earlier made such an inadvertent slip of the tongue. Instead, there was only an open contempt, and . . . was she right in thinking, a suspicion of having expected no better?

If she was correct, just why the latter should have been present, Mallory couldn't fathom, but unaccountably it was that more than her own discomfiture which seemed to have the greatest effect on her, and which eventually, under cover of her stepfather's continuing coversation, had her glancing covertly in the younger man's direction once more in search of a clue.

' . . . and I'll just get us something colder to drink while we discuss it,' she suddenly realised Ward was saying, and already heading for the kitchen.

With his departure, all Mallory's previous puzzlings fled as her disconcertment promptly returned in full force on finding herself alone with Bren Dalton once again, and she shifted from one foot to the other uncomfortably.

'Look, I'm sorry for not explaining exactly who I

was, but I really only meant it as a joke,' she defended herself with a conciliatory half-smile, deciding that, if the air had to be cleared, it was undoubtedly better done sooner than later.

'Yes, well, if that's what passes for a joke in your circles . . .' Bren shrugged dismissively, his hard-set expression showing no signs of relenting.

Ignoring his reference to her 'circles'—whatever that was supposed to imply!—Mallory resorted to a little attacking herself. 'Then maybe you shouldn't have been so quick to jump to conclusions in the first place!'

'Conclusions you were more than willing to promote, I might remind you!'

'Although only *after* you first made them!'

His mouth curved sardonically. 'So what else was I supposed to think on suddenly discovering someone like you swanning about the veranda as if you owned the place?'

Mallory sucked in a resentful breath. 'I was not swanning about, I was merely sunning myself!'

She was abruptly subjected to a thorough survey that left her feeling distinctly shaken. And that surprised her. After all, she was accustomed to being critically appraised—by experts!

'Mmm, you look as if you could do with some,' Bren mocked. 'Have you been sick or something?'

'No, I have not been sick!' Indignation came to her rescue. 'It's simply preferable for models not to have suntans, that's all!'

'So why the apparent attempt to acquire one now?'

Abruptly aware of the conversation somehow being diverted, and the shrewdness that prompted the question—not to mention her own unwillingness actually to come face to face with her reasons—Mallory waved one hand flusteredly. 'Because I—I just felt like it!' She went on swiftly. 'And—and precisely what did you mean by 'someone like me', anyway?'

'Oh, don't play ignorant with me, sweetheart!' He took her aback with the scathing nuance in his retort. 'You've been trading on your looks and figure—very sucessfully, too, according to Ward—for some years now, apparently!'

Although taking exception to his choice of terms, Mallory still let it pass in favour of making her own point. 'That still doesn't automatically make me someone's bed-mate!' She paused, an irrepressible smile beginning to catch at the corners of her mouth. 'And especially not of someone like Ward who, from your own knowledge of him, you should have known wasn't really likely to be into that kind of relationship. He's far too traditional in outlook.'

Bren's hard features grew mockingly disparaging. 'It's also a known fact that a man's attitudes can change radically once a woman's involved!'

As his had once done—to his regret? Mallory wondered. Was it a woman, then, who had caused that conflict of sentiments she could see in the lines of his mouth? And as a result made him immediately suspicious of her reason for being at Avalon? It was an intersting theory, and one she discovered she would have liked to pursue, but doubted now was the time to do so. In lieu, she shrugged and sought a slightly different tack.

'Well, surely you must have known Ward had a stepdaughter. I mean, when Banfield's took over the property, there must have been at least some mention made regarding his family.'

'And do you think I've nothing more important to

occupy my time than to recollect every employee's family members?' he countered in a voice heavy with sarcasm. 'As disappointing as you may find it, in view of the fact that you haven't been around since we bought the property, I had, to put it quite bluntly, completely forgotten you even existed!'

Mallory pulled a rueful face, and suspected that he was never anything but forthright! She tried again doggedly. 'I still could just have been visitor, or—or . . .'

'Of Ward's? At your age?' he cut in scornfully. 'Doesn't that seem a trifle far-fetched, even to you?'

She supposed it was somewhat unlikely, but at the same time . . . 'You still shouldn't have jumped to conclusions,' she insisted. 'One of these days you could find such a reaction having dire consequences.'

'Although nowhere near as disastrous if I didn't immediately believe the worst!' Bren had no compunction in shooting back.

Implying, once again, where women were concerned? Or did he apply that seemingly ever-ready cynicism to all aspects of life? Her stepfather's eventual return with a can of beer in each hand, and the two men's ensuing departure for the small office next to the breakfast-room—to set the offical seal on Ward's resignation, as it were, Mallory surmised heavily—abruptly put an end to her speculations, if only temporarily.

They returned inexorably when she, in turn, set about preparing their evening meal, so that by the time the men at last emerged, she quickly sought whatever information she could from her stepfather while Bren was otherwise engaged in unloading his vehicle. None the less, her first and most anxious query related to her home, not surprisingly.

'So it's finalised, we're—you're—leaving Avalon?' she hazarded with a dismal sigh.

Ward nodded, his expression apologetic. 'I'm sorry, pet.'

Her attempt at a resigned smile in response wasn't very successful. 'Oh, I guess I'll get over it,' she claimed, trying to make him feel better about it at least. 'As one door shuts, another one opens, so they say. Who knows what might be waiting just around the corner.'

'That's the spirit, he lauded, hugging her to his side affectionately. 'And in the meantime, why don't you come with Bren and me when we go over the place in the next few days, hmm? It's been a long time since we've been over all of it together—it may even be our last opportunity to do so—and Bren has some great ideas in mind that he's contemplating putting into practice. Who knows, you may even want to add some comments yourself.' His lips twisted obliquely. 'As well as perhaps understanding just why I figured it was time for me to get out of farming.'

'Because they are wanting to diversify, as you thought they might?'

'And how!' Ward rolled his eyes expressively. 'But that's not all of it either, not by a long shot!

Less interested in the plans than the man making them, Mallory chose her words carefully. 'So Bren's a sort of ideas man for Banfield's, is he?'

'Oh, a bit more than that,' she was advised with a chuckle. 'He's innovator, troubleshooter . . . and the head of their rural division! Not just for Victoria either, I might add, but for all their properties—and there's quite a number of them—no matter what

State they're in. He's got plenty of nous, that one, I can tell you!'

'Then if he's in charge, how can he afford to remain here for the amount of time he apparently intends to?'

'Probably can't,' with another laugh. 'But he'll make time if he considers it necessary. That's also why we now have an answering machince connected to the telephone, the same as all the other Banfield properties. He'll probably be on the phone most of this evening. It gets a lot of use whenever he's here, believe me!'

Mallory nodded thoughtfully. 'If he does the same with all their properties, he must be away from home a lot,' she reflected.

'I don't think he has any complaints about the amount of time he has to spend in the bush rather than the city.'

She made a pretence of looking for something in one of the overhead kitchen cupboards. 'And is his—umm—wife, equally satisfied with that state of affairs?'

'More likely, it's probably the reason he doesn't have one,' speculated Ward in wry tones.

'I see.' Strangely, Mallory experienced a peculiar spurt of satisfaction. Nor had it been a wife, evidently, who had caused that cynicism—as she had contemplated might have been the case. 'Then if he prefers the bush, do I take it that means he also originally came from there and not the city?' she probed further.

'Mmm, outback New South, I think he happened to mention once,' her stepfather confirmed co-operatively. 'I've no idea exactly whereabouts, though. He doesn't give much away about himself, or his background, at all, in fact.'

A statement that only seemed to pique Mallory's interest more. 'Although he does seem relatively young to have so much responsibility. Has he worked for Banfield's for very long, do you know?'

Disappointingly, it transpired that he didn t. 'No, I only know that he was certainly there and in charge when they took over Avalon. Apart from that, I've no idea.' Suddenly, his blue eyes took on a teasing glint. 'So why all the interest, anyway? He attracts you, does he?'

Swallowing at the unexpected turn the conversation had taken, Mallory half turned away, as if it required her undivided attention to place their plates just so on the serving-bench. 'Well, I won't say he's not physically attractive,' she allowed with what she hoped was a convincing display of nonchalance. How could she have said otherwise? He *was* attractive . . . damnably attractive! And her stepfather was neither blind nor stupid! 'But I was just curious, that's all. Don't forget, having employers moving on to the property for days at a time is all new to me. When Clyde Gilroy owned it, we rarely used to see him from one year to the next!'

'Yes, things have certainly changed . . . and in more ways than one,' Ward had no hesitation in conceding. 'And as you'll undoubtedly come to realise during the next few days when you hear what Bren has in mind.'

And realise Mallory definitely did as the ensuing days passed. If a change from Avalon's traditional crop was necessary—and it appeared that her stepfather and Bren Dalton both considered it was—then Bren Dalton obviously didn't believe in

half-measures. And in spite of her initial
resistance—she had always considered Avalon the
perfect property just as it was—Mallory gradually
found herself becoming more and more interested
in, and excited by, the unlimited possibilities
provided by planning on such a large scale and with
such scope. In fact, her disappointent at having to
leave Avalon even became greater—something
she wouldn't previously have believed was
possible—simply because she knew she wouldn't be
there to see it all come to fruition.

That it could only have been undertaken by a
corporation like Banfield's, with sufficient financial
resources to fund the operation, was immediately
evident. As was the fact that the capital expenditure
involved required a larger property than even
Avalon—the largest by far in the district already—to
make it worth while. Consequently, Mallory wasn't
altogether surprised when it was disclosed that
negotiations were already under way to purchase
another two adjoining ones in the drier country to
the west.

What she found most absorbing, however, were
the different farming practices themselves that were
to be utilised, from the contouring of the soil in order
to maximise the benefit of the rain they did receive to
the diversification of their usual cereals with grain
legumes and oilseeds, and perhaps the most radical
of all, the plan to produce a variety of crops at
one time for assorted, specialised, alternative
markets; the whole being geared to stock-market
requirements and prices rather than traditional
custom.

Nor was the grazing side of the operation to be
forgotten, it seemed. Upgrading their present flock

had also been discussed, as well as methods of pasture improvement, and even the experiment of growing carpet instead of apparel wool on one of the other properties.

In other words, if it had prospects, Bren was willing to give it his consideration, and he had a good record behind him of successful projects he had instigated, so Mallory was told by her stepfather.

'Well, he certainly knows land, and farming—of every type, it appears—I'll give him that,' she conceded after their last particularly long and tiring day identifying those lower areas of Avalon that received the rainfall run-off, so that the location for the necessary earth-contouring could be noted. 'Lord, he lost me completely on some of those more exotic crops he was talking about today. I've never heard of half of them before!'

'Nor had I a few of them, but I'm glad to say that's something I won't have to worry about,' responded Ward, meaningfully wry. 'Although I must admit they certainly have some potential by the sound of it.'

'But you still don't want to be a part of any of it,' Mallory stated rather than questioned, and shook her head in disbelief as they made their way from the garage to the homestead. Bren had already gone on ahead to answer the imperative summons of the phone. She continued enthusiastically, 'I think it would be great! I mean, to see all the changes taking place, and then new crops producing. It would be fantastic to know that you had been involved in it all!'

'At your age, more than likely,' he agreed. 'But at mine . . .' He shook his head in veto. 'And don't forget either that it will also involve a lot of hard work not only to move into new crops, but to ensure that all their individual diseases and pests—which all have to be learnt and recognised—don't ruin all your efforts in the meantime! It won't be any picnic for whoever takes over as manager here, I can assure you!'

Mallory didn't doubt that for one minute, but it still couldn't dampen her enthusiasm for the project. And besides, she reflected later while showering, with someone like Bren Dalton in charge it was almost impossible to believe it could be anything but successful. Not only because of his past record, but because his very demeanour—calm, assured, and overwhelmingly in control—seemed to inspire confidence.

'Well, we certainly managed to cover some ground today.' It was Ward who brought the matter conversationally to the fore during dinner that evening. He sent Bren an enquiring glance. 'How many more days do you reckon it will take before you've all the information you need?'

'Oh, probably only a couple, or three at the most,' the younger man replied casually. 'Most of it's done now, of course, but there's a few things I wouldn't mind checking before I leave—just to make sure.'

'And then?' asked Ward, and Mallory waited interested for the reply.

Bren flexed a broad shoulder. 'Then I return to Melbourne to co-ordinate all the information, and make the necessary arrangements so that the work can proceed as soon as this year's harvest is in, and the purchase of the other properties is finalised.'

'And after that?' put in Mallory, wanting to know more.

'I go on vacation for a month,' he said, in somewhat mockingly squashing accents.

Mallory grimaced, despite not really having expected him to answer a question of hers, at least, in any other fashion. It wasn't that he had exactly ignored her presence since their first unfortunate meeting, but apart from a few derisive looks and similarly sardonically voiced remarks, he hadn't precisely gone out of his way to acknowledge her either!

As a result, an incorrigible imp of mischief now had her persisting, 'To anywhere in particular?'

'Yes.' It was cool, firm, and final.

Only Mallory wasn't prepared to see it that way. 'And where might that be?' she persevered with assumed innocence, purposely disregarding her stepfather's shake of the head that suggested she desist.

To her surprise, Bren's previously caustic gaze became shuttered. 'Somewhere private!' he bit out in a menacingly low tone.

That closed expression had Mallory's slender brows drawing together slightly, her curiosity really whetted now. The more so on recalling her stepfather's comment about Bren's not giving much away about himself or his background. At the same time she was very much aware of a feeling of having suddenly collided with a brick wall, so that although she would dearly have liked to probe a little further, she strongly suspected it would be more prudent for her not to at the moment. Somewhere private, he had said, and it appeared evident that was how he intended it to remain!

Meanwhile, Ward, plainly in an effort to ensure she didn't proceed, stepped in hastily. 'So when do

you expect to begin advertising for a replacement
manager?' he asked.

With a last narrowed glance in Mallory's
direction—which she returned with an artlessly
limpid smile—Bren gave his attention to the older
man. 'Next week, or thereabouts, most likely. The
interviews to be conducted when I return to work.'

Ward nodded, continuing conversationally, 'And
what sort of a person will you be looking for?
Someone with qualifications from an agricultural
college, or simply someone with practical experience
involving the crops you're interested in?'

For her part, Mallory was surprised at just how
anxiously she found herself waiting on an answer.

However, Bren's mouth merely tilted wryly and
he gave an indeterminate shrug. 'Since it's doubtful
there even are many of the latter—where some of the
crops are concerned, there are only one or two
properties in the whole country, that I know of,
producing them commercially—it may turn out to
be one of the former,' he imparted casually. 'Not
that formal qualifications will be strictly necessary,
of course. It could just as easily be someone who
simply has the required management skills and the
ability to learn as they go along, by trial and error.
We're well aware that experimentation of this kind
has its pitfalls, but . . . it also has the potential to be
extremely profitable if approached in the right
manner . . . like, with general farming experience
and a judicious application of plain common sense.'

'In that case, I would hereby like to apply for the
position!' The words seemed to tumble from
Mallory's lips of their own volition, even before she
was aware of having thought them. But once said,
she knew she had no desire to alter or retract

them either. Now she also knew why her increasingly darkening skin—much darker than she had originally intended—had occasioned her so little concern. Subconsciously, at least, she had already made up her mind not to return to modelling. More important, though, it was the perfect opportunity for her to remain at Avalon. As considerate as it was of Cecily and Ward to invite her, she just didn't *want* to live in town, even with them. But when nothing but a stunned silence followed her abrupt declaration, she promptly followed it up with a challenging survey of the two men at the table and an equally defiant, 'Well?'

Momentarily, her stepfather continued to look lost for words, but Bren burst out laughing. The fact that it was the first time she had seen or heard him laugh—such a pure, deep sound, and so attractive—did little for either her confidence or her composure. That it should also have been totally amused—not a trace of mockery present, as she might have expected—only served to nettle her. Sarcasm she could have withstood, but unadulterated mirth she found disparaging in the extreme.

'But—but . . . your modelling?' In the end it was Ward who spluttered into bemused speech first.

'Mmm, I'd suggest you keep to pirouetting on catwalks, sweetheart,' added Bren, a definite sardonic inflection beginning to surface now.

'You forgot to mention smiling for the cameras, too!' Mallory was quick to round on him acidly. 'And why should I stay with either of them, anyway? Is it so improbable that I might prefer to do something else?'

'In this instance, yes!' Bren had no compunction in stating in categorial tones.

'And you would certainly find the wages nothing compared to what you're used to,' put in Ward.

Mallory spared him a partly condemning, partly disappointed glance. She had thought he might have supported her, at least. 'Meaning, money is more important than job-satisfaction?' she gibed.

'Well, you have always seemed more than content with your occupation until now,' he offered excusingly.

'On top of which, I can assure you Banfield's is no philanthropic organisation willing to be conveniently made use of just because you've suddenly decided it might be fun to play at being a farmer for a while!' Bren inserted on an abrasive, derogatory note.

Mallory's amethyst eyes sparkled militantly. 'And I wasn't aware I had suggested that it should be a philanthropic organisation! Do you honestly think that after having lived here for as long as I have I know nothing about farming? Who on earth do you think used to do the majority of the bookwork, help with the seeding and stripping, join in with the mustering and drenching of the sheep, drive the machinery . . . and repair it when necessary?' She paused, breathing deeply, the look on his face making her temper rise. 'And if you don't believe I can do mechanical repairs, then ask Ward, he'll tell you! Go on, ask him!'

'Mmm, it's true enough,' her stepfather volunteered without having to be requested. 'As was all the other. I have to admit there's not much on the place she doesn't know about.'

'Although actually making the decisions, and helping to carry them out, are two entirely different matters, of course,' Bren said subtly.

'Well, all those people who have eventually become managers had to make the change some time!' Mallory defended.

The incline of Bren's head was acknowledging, but not his comment. 'Although not necessarily at the Banfield Corporation's expense,' he drawled. Then, pushing back his chair and starting to rise to his feet, his gaze moved to Ward. 'And now, if you'll excuse me, I have a few phone-calls to return, and another couple to make before it gets too late.' He turned from the table and began making for the office.

Mallory swung round to stare after him disbelievingly. 'But I haven't finished yet!' she protested in a stormy voice.

'I have!' came the all too significant reply over a wide shoulder before he disappeared from the room.

Resentment flared, and for a moment she was tempted to go after him and force the issue, but after a while reason began to prevail and her indignation found an outlet through her rapidly drumming fingers on the table-top instead. If he thought he could dismiss the matter that easily, he was in for a shock, she fumed. She was deadly serious about wanting the position, and if that meant biding her time until later—when he might perhaps have become more used to the idea—then that was what she would do.

Gaining her own feet now, Mallory started to clear the table mechanically, her features turning rueful when her eyes met her stepfather's on collecting his dessert bowl to add to the others.

'You weren't exactly supportive, were you?' she sighed.

Ward's lips curved graphically. 'Maybe if you

hadn't sprung it on me quite so unexpectedly . . .'
He shrugged, and then hesitated. 'Although I'm not
sure I would have been altogether in favour of it, in
any event.'

'But why not? Do you think I'm incapable of
doing anything but parading up and down a
catwalk, or facing a camera?' She couldn't keep the
hurt out of her voice.

'No, of course I don't!' he tried to reassure her,
smiling gently. 'But it would have been such a
contrast, and . . .'

'You keep referring to it in the past tense!'
Mallory cut in to remonstrate ironically.

'Well, isn't it?' he countered on a dry note, his
grey brows lifting. 'I thought Bren had made his
feelings on the matter very clear.'

'So, good for Bren!' she quipped. 'It just so
happens that I *don't* consider the matter closed.'

'Now, pet,' Ward hastened to urge caution.
'You're not going to do yourself any good by
crossing swords with him. Take my word for it, he's
not the type of man to be browbeaten into changing
his mind.' Abruptly, he grinned. 'Or, as I've known
you do with others—including myself,' he inserted
ruefully, 'allowing you to overcome his objections
with a few of your beautiful smiles and a charmingly
sabotaging manner.'

A roguish smile made an appearance. 'Although
there's no harm in trying, is there?' Not that she
actually intended to employ either method. Simply
cool, calm reason. A sudden thought occured and
her expression sobered a little. 'You've no objection
to that, have you?' Bren was still his boss, after all.

He gave a brief shake of his head. 'Not on the
basis that it might rebound disadvantageously on me

in some way, if that's what you're thinking. I can't see that being a course Bren's likely to take. However . . .' he eyed her expressively, 'on personal grounds . . .'

'I know!' she broke in rapidly, making a whimsical moue. 'You would rather I continued with modelling—or something equally ornamental—instead of grubbing around in a paddock or chasing after a mob of sheep on a motor-bike . . . right?' Without giving him a chance to comment, she went on hurriedly, 'But I'd already told you I was losing my interest in modelling, and although at the time I had no idea what I wanted to replace it with, after these last few days, now I do know! I don't want to return to the city, any city. I want to stay here and work on the land. If it's a choice between working under hot lights in a stuffy studio, and working outdoors in the heat of the sun, I'll take the sun any day! I've had my fling with the glamorous high-life, and I admit I enjoyed it, but now I'd like to do something a little more . . . well, worth while *and* challenging. And I could make a go of it, I'm sure I could!'

'Well, if confidence and enthusiasm count for anything . . .' Ward smiled and released a resigned breath. 'OK, if it's what you *really* want, I'll support you in whatever way I can. And you know that I'll always be available to give advice, if it's required.' Pausing, an oblique slope caught at his lips. 'All provided, of course, that you're as successful in persuading Bren to grant his approval.'

'He will!' Mallory predicted, but with an air of assurance that was a touch simulated. He just had to! she appended silently. It meant too much to her even to contemplate defeat. 'When all's said and done, he did say that it was quite probable they would merely hire someone with general farming experience and some common sense, and I consider I qualify on both those counts.' She tossed her long hair over her shoulder in a gesture of resolve. 'I'll go and put my case to him after I've finished clearing away and loading the dishwasher.' That appliance, along with a couple of others, was one of the benefits of the Banfield Corporation's having taking over the property, she had soon discovered after her return.

'I'd make certain he's finished his business calls first, though, or he may not view the interruption favourably,' her stepfather warned.

'Mmm, it sure is business, business, business, all the way as far as he's concerned, isn't it? Is he bucking for promotion, or someone else's job?'

'No, it's merely a case of loyalty,' Ward said, but with just enough censure in his voice for her to realise she had said the wrong thing, and to have her half smiling regretfully as a result.

'Sorry, but loyalty isn't a characteristic I've had much experience with of late. The modelling game's more cut-throat than anything.' Her forehead creased. 'But does he also have to be quite so serious all the time? I mean, apart from an ironic,' mentally she substituted, sardonic, 'quirk or two to his mouth, he doesn't exactly smile often either.'

'Maybe he's just basically a serious person.'

Oddly, Mallory found that difficult to accept. 'Or maybe there's a specific reason,' she hazarded softly.

Ward shrugged. 'If there is, I don't know him well enough to know what it could be.' He unknowingly destroyed her hopes of his being able to supply the information.

'Oh, well, I guess it must be as you said, then,' she could do little else but concede, and gathering up the bowls she headed for the kitchen.

As it turned out, it was some time after Mallory had finished in the kitchen before she thought it advisable to approach Bren in the office. Only on the last two occasions when she had listened briefly outside the door for the sound of his voice had she been greeted by silence, a sign that he might at last have concluded his business on the phone.

Now, armed with a mug of steaming coffee—whether as a peace offering or a cover to disguise her reason for being there, she wasn't too sure—she knocked and entered the room with a smile firmly in place.

'You've been in here so long I thought you might like something to drink,' she said casually, crossing the floor and depositing the mug beside him on the small desk that was strewn with papers.

'Thank you.' Bren dipped his head fractionally in acknowledgement. 'It has been a long evening.'

After a few seconds spent surveying the room in order to fill in time, Mallory subsided gracefully on to a chair beside the windows. 'You must have been very busy.'

His alert blue eyes never wavered from her face for a minute. 'I still am,' he drawled.

Swallowing, she ignored the hint to leave, and tilted her head consideringly instead. 'You work too hard, you know. You should take it easier occasionally.' The beginnings of a teasing smile caught at the edges of her soft lips. 'After all, you, know, as the saying goes, what all work and no play does to you . . .'

'So what are you suggesting? That I should take time off to . . . play . . . with you?' he queried mockingly.

She had to concede the idea wasn't unappealing. 'I guess that all depends on the form of . . . play . . . you have in mind,' she replied in unexpectedly husky tones, watching him through the glossy veil of her luxuriant lashes.

For a time Bren's continuing regard was inscrutable, and then a cynical sweep curved his mouth. 'And is that how you always go about achieving your ends?'

Mallory blinked. 'Meaning?'

His features hardened imperceptibly. 'I do realise why you're here, sweetheart, but the answer is still, no!'

'But—but that remark had nothing to do with it!' she immediately denied, appalled, on grasping his meaning. In truth, at the time she had temporarily forgotten all about her reason for being there. 'The same as yours didn't! At least . . .' her gaze turned doubtful, 'I presume it didn't.'

'Your presumption's correct!'

'Yours isn't,' she insisted on a gentle note.

Bren released a heavy breath and shook his head. 'No matter, the answer still hasn't changed.'

'But why?' Her voice started to rise.

His mouth levelled. 'You're wasting your time—and mine—Mallory!'

On the verge of letting fly with a pungent quip, she only just managed to control it in time. Cool, calm reason, she had promised herself, she recollected. 'Then I'm sorry, but I still believe I'm entitled to an explanation at least,' she submitted steadily. 'Is it because I'm a female?'

He made a dismissive gesture with one hand. 'Although normally on family properties, there are other women successfully running farming ventures,' he allowed.

Damn him, that had been *her* next argument! 'But you obviously don't consider me capable of doing the same here!'

Bren raised a sardonic brow. 'Well, could you?'

'I don't see why not!' Mallory retorted on a somewhat flaring note.

'Well, I do! And since I'm the one who not only has to select the applicant to fill the position, but also accept the responsibility for that decision, I think that's fairly important, don't you?' Sarcasm really began making itself felt now. 'Because accepting responsibility for you, my sweet, is something I am extremely loath to do! You have an unfortunate penchant for being misleading; you have no proven management, or if it comes to that, farming skills; in view of your previous less-than-vigorous life-style, there's no guarantee you even have the physical ability to do the work; and just to top it all, I wouldn't put it past you to resign the minute the going got a little tough!' He inhaled deeply. 'So now you've had your explanation, would you mind letting me get back to my work?' He dropped his gaze to the papers on the desk in front of him.

Mallory glared at his down-bent head but refused to budge. 'And so could any man you employed resign for the same reasons!' she declared fiercely. Then, choosing the point she considered most relevant, 'While as for management and farming skills . . . well, just because I haven't actually been in charge here, it doesn't automatically mean I don't possess any! And nor does the fact that I happen to

have been otherwise occupied for the last few years
mean I don't know as much about growing
wheat—and the necessary rotational crops—as
Ward does!'

After a long silence, broken only by her quickened
breathing, Bren finally lifted his head again, slowly,
long sufferingly. 'Except that, it appears to have
escaped your notice that we don't intend growing
much wheat in future,' he drawled derisively. 'And
you have no experience whatever with any of the
crops we are contemplating planting.'

'Neither does Ward!' she rushed to point out. A
certain hint of mockery found its way on to her
features. 'So what were you planning to do if he
hadn't resigned? Fire him?'

'You're forgetting, he at least had a track record
in other areas. If you want to work on the land, then
I suggest you get a position as a jillaroo somewhere.
But . . . Banfield's are not, I repeat *not*, ' his voice
started to harden, 'paying for you to learn on one of
their properties!'

'Although they are willing to pay for someone else
to do so, apparently!' Mallory threw back at him in
resentful tones. 'What's more, *you're forgetting,*'
satirically emphasised, 'I have already done the
equivalent of seven years' jillarooing on *this*
property!' Rising to her feet, she strove for a more
moderate tone as she crossed to the desk. 'Look, you
could at least give me a trial, couldn't you? I mean,
I'm available to start right away, and it would save
you the cost of advertising, and relieve you of the
need to spend time interviewing applicants. Is
merely a trial really asking too much?' Her violet
eyes held his eloquently.

It seemed an interminable time that their gazes

remained locked, and Mallory could only hope and pray he was reconsidering, but then a muscle rippled at the side of Bren's jaw and he arched a contemptuous brow. 'Simply because you decided on a whim that that's what you have a fancy to do?' he grated corrosively. 'Or could it be just another of your little jokes, hmm? Because you think it will be diverting? After all, you can always trade on your looks to get you out of trouble if it suddenly loses its fascination, can't you? The same as you're obviously trying to do with your beautiful, pleading eyes right now! In fact, you've doubtless become so used to turning them to your account that you think they're an automatic passport to whatever you want!' He sucked in a hissing breath. 'Well, I'm sorry to disappoint you, sweetheart, but this time the joke's on you, because you're not conning me with those practised tactics! The answer is still, no . . . and that's final!'

Mallory had been so unprepared for his scornful attack that, momentarily, she was too shaken to do anything but stare at him in disbelief. But as his words began to sink in, her eyes smouldered rebelliously and her rounded breasts rose and fell sharply. 'Conning you!' she expostulated fierily, all thought of calm rationality gone now. 'I was begging you—at the expense of my pride and principles—for just a chance, no matter how small, to prove myself! And if you weren't such a dyed-in-the-wool cynical bastard, you might have managed to grasp that fact . . . although even that's doubtful!' Her eyes widened sarcastically. 'But if you think I'm going to allow you to discriminate against me, or deter me because I didn't immediately correct *your* misassumption on the day you arrived, then you can think again! I am going to apply for the post of manager here, and I'll do so by going over your head if that's what's required in order to receive a fair hearing!'

'Oh?' He quirked a taunting, totally unconcerned brow. 'Over my head to whom, might I ask?'

Yes, she supposed he could afford to look sardonically complacent in view of his being the highest authority in Banfield's rural division, but she wasn't finished yet. 'To Joshua Banfield himself, if that's what it takes!' she threw back at him. 'And that's no idle threat either, if that's what you're thinking, because I do happen to know him! In fact, it's amazing at times just how many influential figures one does become acquainted with in the modelling profession.' She allowed herself the satisfaction of sparing him a triumphant glance.

Not that it had any visible effect. 'Although you may discover it requires even more than *your* looks, no matter how well you think you know him, to get in to see him. Especially on such a, to him at least, minor matter as the filling of one relatively insignificant position,' Bren mocked.

'We'll see.' Mallory felt sufficiently confident to goad him with a smile in return, and left the room with a light step. Little did he know, but she had carefully refrained from revealing her strongest weapon!

CHAPTER THREE

THE following morning, Mallory cried off from accompanying the men over the property with the excuse that she thought she might go into town with Janet Crowley in order to do a bit of shopping and to look up some old friends, as she hadn't yet been into Nyandra since her return.

It was a statement that had Bren eyeing her measuringly, but since it was a known fact that Janet did always go into town on Fridays, he eventually shrugged and left with her stepfather without saying a word. However, as soon as they were out of sight, it wasn't towards Dick and Janet's house that Mallory hurried, but into the office in order to use the phone.

In all honesty she couldn't really claim to *know* Joshua Banfield—she had merly met him on a couple of occasions, that was all—so Bren had more than likely been correct the previous evening when he had claimed she would find it difficult to see the head of the Banfield Corporation.

The one thing she did have going for her, though, and which she hadn't divulged, was the fact that Duncan Amery—for whom she had previously worked, and the owner of one of the largest modelling-agencies in Melbourne—happened to be Joshua Banfield's nephew. And Duncan was normally very obliging! She only hoped he didn't object to her ringing him so early at his home, but she was anxious to catch him before he left for the day.

Dialling the number, Mallory waited anxiously while the phone rang the other end—what if he was away somewhere?—and then gave a thankful sigh when the receiver was lifted and Duncan's familiar voice sounded in her ear.

'Hello, Duncan!' she responded. 'It's . . . '

'Mallory!' he interrupted to exclaim enthusiastically. 'I'd know that sexy voice anywhere! When did you arrive back home? I though you were still in the States. Are you back for good?' The questions came in whirlwind fashion, without giving her time to answer them. 'Look, if you're after work, I know just the thing for you! *Vogue* is preparing a five-page spread on autumn brides—you know the sort of thing—and I just know they would jump at the chance to use you! Or maybe you feel like a trip to one of the Barrier Reef islands. I've got an assignment that's just perfect for you, and . . . '

'Duncan, I am not looking for work!' Mallory was forced into saying loudly in order to cut him short, even as she stifled her laughter. He was never any different when work was involved.

'Oh, you mean you haven't the time before you wing out again?' he surmised in strongly disappointed tones.

'No-o,' she amended slowly. 'Actually, I won't be going back.' She paused. 'In fact, I'm giving up modelling altogether.'

There was a stunned silence, as she had suspected there might be. Even if only temporarily. 'Sweetie, you can't be serious!' he ejaculated. 'You're at peak of your career! It would be a crime for you to give it up completely! Look, if it's getting too much, why not concentrate on one aspect . . . say, the photographic work?' His voice started to become more excited. 'Now in that regard, I know of . . . '

'Duncan!' she had to shout in order to call a halt once more. 'I want to do something else altogether.'

'You do?' His bewilderment was evident even from so far away.

'Mmm, I want to work on the land, and . . . '

'On the land!' Duncan cut in on an incredulous note. 'On the *land!* Have you gone mad? I know you come from the country, and all that, but I think you must have been out in the sun for too long!'

Mallory laughed. 'No, I've just realised that I haven't been out in the sun enough these last few years.'

'But—but . . . sweetie, you're having me on, aren't you?'

'No, I was never more serious, as a matter of fact. It's something I very much want to do.'

There was another silence. 'My God, I think I'm beginning to believe you,' he conceded on a sigh.

'I'm glad, because it's in that connection that I rang you.' She hesitated. 'I was hoping you might do me a favour.'

'Any time, sweetie, you know that,' he offered with his usual amiability. He started to laugh. 'Although God only knows how I can help if it's connected with the land. That's never really been my scene.'

'But Joshua Banfield is your uncle, isn't he?'

'Oh, that's the connection, is it? Yes, he's my uncle. So what can I do for you concerning him?'

'I know he's a very busy man, but . . . would it be possible for you to arrange an appointment for me to

see him this afternoon, please?' she enquired
anxiously. And biting at her lip, 'I'm afraid it would
have to be lateish, too, because I have to catch the
bus to Melbourne and it won't arrive until five
thirty.' Unfortunately Ward's car would have to
have been at the garage in town having some repairs
done, and she couldn't take the ute because he and
Bren were already using that.

'No matter, I'm sure I'll be able to arrange
something.' Duncan predicted confidently. 'If I get
on to it straight away I'll catch him before he leaves
for the office. Give me your number and I'll ring you
back, OK?'

Complying with his request, Mallory went on
earnestly, 'Thanks, Duncan, I really do appreciate
your help. This is very important to me.'

'No sweat. What are friends for?' he countered
genially before ringing off.

While waiting for his return call, Mallory
hurriedly set about packing a few things to take with
her. No matter what time her appointment, the bus
schedule determined that she would have to stay
overnight, Then she began on a note for her
stepfather, advising him of her whereabouts—although not the exact reasons for her
journey—all the while keeping her fingers crossed
that he and Bren wouldn't return to the homestead
before their normal hour. Bren, she was certain,
would immediately guess her intention, and with the
trip being much faster by car, he would be off in a
flash in the hope of forestalling her, she didn't
doubt.

She was still writing when the phone rang, and she
picked, or rather snatched, up the receiver swiftly.

'You're all set,' Duncan's cheerful voice advised

on her answering, and had her expelling a relieved breath. 'Although he couldn't manage it at the office, I'm sorry. Apparently he's going to be flat out like a lizard drinking all day there. However, there's a corporation do on this evening—you know, for the approaching festive season and all that—and he says he'll be able to give you some time then, about seven, if that suits you.'

If it suited *her?* Duncan must really have put in some effort on her behalf. 'Are you sure *he* doesn't mind seeing me then?' Mallory countered apprehensively.

'No, he was quite amenable,' he allayed her worries with a blithe nonchalance. 'As a matter of fact, he says he remembers you—how could anyone forget you?—and he's quite interested to discover why you're wanting to see him.' He paused briefly. 'Do I get any clues?'

'I'll tell you when I get to Melbourne,' she said. 'It's rather complicated, and if I don't hurry I'll miss my lift into town.' It wouldn't be long before Janet would be leaving. 'That is, I take it I will be seeing you?'

'As if I would let the opportunity pass! Besides, I was going to the party, anyway. So don't forget to bring something glam to wear, and I'll pick you up around six-thirty. Oh, where will you be staying, by the way?'

'One or other hotel, I suppose. I hadn't really thought about it.'

'Why not make it the Garden State?' he suggested, mentioning one of the newest and best hotels in the city. 'That's where the party's being held.'

It seemed a satisfactory arrangement. 'Suits me.

And I'll see you there around six-thirty.'

'I'm looking forward to it.'

Quickly now, Mallory finished her note to Ward, added something glam—as Duncan had recommended—to her case, and changed into a casually comfortable outfit for her bus journey. Initially, the time of her appointment had caused her some consternation, but she consoled herself with the thought that, even if her stepfather and Bren did return a little early, her interview with Joshua Banfield should still be concluded at least an hour before Bren could possibly arrive.

Nevertheless, she continued to experience moments of nervousness throughout the day. First, as she waited in Nyandra until midday for the bus to arrive, then during the lengthy journey to Melbourne, and lastly, but by no means least, as she prepared for her meeting with Joshua Banfield. She remembered him as a rather distinguished-looking man with iron-grey hair, reasonably tall, though only sparingly built, but possessed of an asute pair of grey eyes. That his brain must be as shrewd was evident in the way he had turned the family corporation into one of the most substantial and progressive in the country after taking control on the death of his father. Just the thought of trying to convince such a man to overrule one of his own managers was now beginning to appear foolhardy, if not plain futile.

Duncan's comments when he arrived to collect her went a long way to returning her to the right frame of mind, however.

'You look utterly fabulous!' he complimented her as he surveyed her plain but very chic black chiffon dress. Her long hair she had simply caught back at the nape of her neck with a large chiffon bow. Her only jewellery was a pair of long pear-drop earrings. 'But then, with your face, how could you ever look anything else?'

'Except that when seeking a position on a property in the bush, I suspect that could be one of my biggest drawbacks,' Mallory commented with a rueful and somewhat tentative half-smile as, by common consent, they left the room and made for the lift.

Duncan merely shook his head, decisively, in veto. 'So that's why you want to see him, is it? Well, I'll give you a word of advice. Forget the ''fair lady'' bit, because a faint heart never won anything! So if it's as important to you as you implied it was, go for it, sweetie, for all you're worth!' And as they entered the lift, 'Take a hint from one who knows Joshua Banfield. Audacity is far more likely to impress him than timidity.'

So it was that when they reached the appropriate floor and, passing the wide doorway leading to the ballroom where the party was already in progress came to the room where her meeting with Joshua Banfield was to take place, Mallory was resolved to put her best foot forward, to leave no stone unturned, no argument unused, in order to achieve the desired outcome.

And it seemed she was successful, because when she emerged from the room some forty-five minutes later she had Joshua Banfield's approval for her employment on a six-month trial basis. The only stipulation he had insisted upon was that for the first three months her employment should be under Bren's direct supervision, and not her stepfather's, as she had proposed.

Just how Bren would react to that proviso Mallory really didn't care to speculate, and it was actually far from her thoughts as she smiled in relieved satisfaction on closing the door behind her and prepared to seek out Duncan. His appearance from the ballroom promptly sent trickles of apprehension slithering down her spine, and she replaced her pleased expression with one of dismay and consternation on recognising the man beside him.

Bren! Dressed in a beautifully tailored dark suit, he looked most striking—and, on noting her initial delighted expression, fit to kill! By contrast, Duncan appeared to find something amusing in the situation, for beneath his shock of bright red hair his blue eyes crinkled with a lively humour.

Ignoring him, Mallory swallowed convulsively and came to a dead halt, her eyes huge as they concentrated warily on the taller man's approach. 'Bren, I—I'm . . .' she began falteringly on their reaching her, and she was summarily silenced by the savagely arresting gesture of one of his hands.

'Don't even begin to *think* of leaving before I get back to you!' he ground out, tight-lipped, his features steel-hard and cold with a fury that had obviously had some time to build up. 'I already feel like slaughtering you with my bare hands, and I might just do so if you put me to the trouble of finding you later, you devious little bitch!' With a contemptuous glare he strode past her to the room still occupied by Joshua Banfield and entered it in a furious fashion.

Mallory chewed at her lip anxiously, and turned to Duncan with a despondent sigh. 'He's not exactly happy with me, is he?'

His mouth shaped wryly. 'As I suspect you already knew he wouldn't be. That was the reason behind your wish for an urgent appointment, hmm?' She nodded, a trifle guiltily, and he continued in the same whimiscal manner, 'You also forgot to mention that Bren had already vetoed the idea.'

Her eyes widened. 'He told you?'

'Uh-huh! We're not precisely strangers, you know. I attend most of the Banfield functions, so there's not many of the staff I'm not acquainted with.'

'Oh!' She hadn't realised, although it did raise the possibility of his being able to provide her with more information regarding Bren Dalton, even if she did have more pressing matters with which to concern herself at present. 'But will he be able to persuade your uncle to change his mind about hiring me, do you think?' she probed nervously. She was more than sure that that was exactly what Bren was presently attempting.

'You did succeed in persuading him to employ you, then.' It was more in the line of an acknowledgement than a question. 'I deduced something of the kind—as Bren evidently did, too,' he added with an expressive half-laugh, 'when I noted your original far from downcast demeanour. However, as to Bren now persuading J.B. to reverse his decision . . . well, I would say it's unlikely. And Bren probably believes so as well, which is more than likely why he is so flaming furious over your little stunt. He also knows that my uncle has a liking for playing his hunches when he's of the opinion someone has potential. After all, it was just such a hunch that had him giving Bren himself greater reponsibility when he discovered him working on one of the corporation's properties, and Bren was only eighteen or so at the time.'

Mallory was interested to store the latter information, but once again she could not allow it to divert her. Although partially reassured by Duncan's assertion of Joshua Banfield's conviction, that did, perforce, raise other points.

'Which simply means that during my—umm— coming confrontation with him he's likely to be even more furious than if he had managed to change your uncle's mind,' she surmised ruefully.

Duncan quirked an explicit brow. 'You didn't realise that when you deliberately set out to cross him?' he countered, humorously dry. His other brow now peaked along with the first. 'Someone with the obvious resolve and fortitude that Bren has?'

'Yes, well, of course I knew he wasn't going to take kindly to the idea,' she allowed, in something of an understatement. 'But I didn't really expect it to be quite so soon. I mean, just how *did* he manage to get here so quickly? I thought I'd at least have some time to prepare myself, as it were, before our next meeting, and . . . .' She came to a halt on seeing a widening smile catching at her companion's lips and pulled a partly reproving, partly helpless face. 'It's not funny, Duncan! You heard what he said he felt like doing to me, and I fail to see what you find so amusing about it all!'

'Mainly, the similarity of the problems you're both suddenly having, I guess,' he supplied with an unrepentant chuckle. 'You, probably for the first time in your life, have come up against a male who evidently isn't about to allow himself to be swayed by that beautiful face of yours . . . and likewise, for once he's come across a female who isn't about to give in willingly to him. And I'm most interested in seeing just what the outcome will be.' He smiled again.

Mallory grimaced. 'Thanks! You make me feel like part of the star turn at the circus! The gladiatorial circus!'

'Well, never mind, you may as well relax and enjoy yourself while you're waiting for it to begin,' Duncan proposed banteringly, beginning to usher her towards the ballroom. 'There's quite a number of people here that you know, at it happens. Not the least of them being Eric Cummings.' He paused prior to their joining the crowd of people who were laughing and conversing in groups, drinking, helping themselves to food from the lavish buffet, or simply circulating. 'He's still very keen on you, you know.'

'He is?' Her winged brows peaked in some surprise. Eric was an aspiring merchant banker, but he had been inclined to be a shade too intense for her liking on occasion, so that she had only attended a few functions with him before she had left for overseas. 'I would have thought he'd forgotten all about me by now.'

Duncan laughed and tapped her under the chin. 'You underrate your effect on people, sweetie,' he claimed as they moved into the throng.

Actually, Mallory was pleasantly surprised by the number of people at the party that she had met previously. A case of having returned to much the same business circles, she supposed. So for a while she was able to relax a little as she renewed acquaintances and made new ones, recollected past happenings and discussed approaching ones, was regaled by what others had been doing during her

absence and in turn relayed her own activities.
Although she was careful not to disclose her
intended one.

'Here—your glass is empty—take this one!' Eric
exchanged Mallory's drained champagne flute for a
full one as a waiter passed. Immediately on sighting
her he had swiftly come to her side and accompanied
her since. 'Whereabouts in Melbourne are you
living now? You must give me your new address and
telephone number,' he went on, drawing her slightly
to one side.

Mallory shook her head. 'I'm sorry, but I don't
have an address in Melbourne. I'm living at home,
in the Wimmera.'

'But you will be moving to the city?' he pressed,
frowning.

'Well—probably not for a while at least,' she
dissembled, looking about her for an excuse to
change the subject. When one occurred, she almost
wished it hadn't as her gaze chanced upon Bren and
Joshua Banfield entering the room.

Momentarily, amethyst eyes connected with
glittering cobalt blue, and the nerves in Mallory's
stomach started to flutter with apprehension. Then
the two men parted company, but somewhat to her
confusion, instead of Bren immedeiately heading in
her direction, as she had fully expected, he set off
across the room to speak to a tall, dark-haired girl
who obviously knew him well, judging by her
familiar manner on greeting him. A girl who was a
fairly well known actress and whom Mallory also
recognised.

'Is Charlene Myers Bren Dalton's girlfriend?' she
turned with a frown to query of Eric, only then
realising that he had been in process of seeking more

answers from her.

'What?' he questioned a trifle vexedly when it became apparent she hadn't heard a word he had said. His gaze followed the direction of hers. 'Dalton's girlfriend? Mmm, I suppose you could say she's the flavour of the month as far as he's concerned.'

'Flavour of the month?'

He shrugged uninterestedly. 'None of his girlfriends seem able to capture his interest for very long.' And eyeing her thoughtfully, 'How come you know Bren Dalton, anyway? It's really only been the last couple of years that he's become part of the Banfield social scene. And then only when he happens to be in town.'

This explained why she had never seen him previously. 'Yes, well, Banfield's took over the property my stepfather manages and Bren's been out there on business this last week,' Mallory said with a preoccupied offhandedness as her attention returned inexorably, anxiously, to the man in question. Was he deliberately keeping her on tenterhooks, or wasn't he intending to speak to her at all now?

'Oh, so you came up with him today, then?' Eric's voice had a flat sound to it.

Mallory almost laughed—hysterically. 'No, I came by bus, as a matter of fact,' she replied as evenly as possible, and gulped hastily at her champagne on seeing Bren at last detach himself from Charlene and turn in her direction. The contours of his face became tight-set and grim as he did so, his posture inflexible and coiled with tension. So she wasn't to escape the full force of his wrath, after all, Mallory deduced nervously. Dreading the thought of his anger perhaps being vented on her in Eric's, or anyone else's, hearing, she spoke quickly over her shoulder to the man beside her. 'I'm sorry, but I'm afraid you'll have to excuse me for a moment. I—I have to see Bren about something.' She set off promptly in an attempt to ensure that their obviously impending confrontation took place in a less crowded area.

'Well, there's no reason I can't come, too, is there?' Eric proposed, already starting to follow her.

She swung back swiftly. In a minute or so Bren would have reached them. 'Except that it happens to be a *private* matter!' she all but snapped in her agitation, and really wasn't in any mood to rue her forthright dismissal when he huffily returned to the group they had just left.

That Bren had indeed been close enough to overhear the exchange became evident with his first scathing words on closing the gap between them. 'Oh, yes, it's all right for you to want to keep the matter private in order to save yourself some embarrassment, isn't it? Although I noticed you suffered no such qualms where I was concerned in running to my boss to do as much damage as you could, you conniving bloody troublemaker!' he gritted. 'But if it's privacy you want, then privacy you can have! Although you may wish there were others around to come to your rescue before I'm through with you!' Catching hold of her arm in an iron grip, he began forcing her along with him as he made for the wide entrance doorway.

In spite of her relief at the thought of escaping the eyes, and ears, of those present, Mallory's gaze was still wary as she glanced up to enquire falteringly, 'Wh-where are we going?'

'To the room on the other side of the hall. Since you couldn't wait to get there before, it seems appropriate, don't you think?' He fixed her with a hard, derisive look.

She moved her head in a helpless gesture. 'I—I'm sorry if I caused trouble for you, Bren, that really wasn't my intention,' she pushed out in a shaky voice.

He made a caustic sound of disbelief. 'The hell it wasn't! But despite all your efforts, it's still nothing I can't or won't be able to handle!'

Mallory was glad of that, at least. Well, she thought she was. That last had had something of an ominous ring to it. She took a deep breath and asked the question that was still uppermost in her mind. 'Mr Banfield didn't reverse his decision about giving me a trial, then?'

His chest rose and fell sharply. 'No, you worked your wiles all too well on him!' he grated, contempt in his words and in his demeanour. Reaching the room he flung open the door, propelled her inside, and slammed the door shut forcefully behind them. 'But then, I guess that's not so surprising! After all, trading on your looks is your business, isn't it, sweetheart? And when coupled with the line you apparently fed him . . . Gee, I bet you even went so far as to offer to sleep with him!'

Apprehension abruptly gave way to indignation. 'I didn't have to!' she flared.

'Meaning . . . you would have done, if it had been necessary?'

'No!' she retorted vehemently. His sarcasm rankled. 'Thankfully, he's not as sceptical as you! He was willing to make a rational judgement!' She sucked in a resentful breath. 'While as for trading on looks . . . I noticed you don't appear to have any objection to Charlene Myers having reached where she is today by doing precisely that!'

Bren's lips curled. 'Possibly because she doesn't go behind anyone's back to achieve her aims, or use her looks for the purpose of obtaining work for which she's patently unsuitable!' he lashed back.

Despite suffering a moment's quilt at his initial words, Mallory held his gaze defiantly. 'Joshua Banfield evidently thinks otherwise,' she dared to point out.

A muscle flickered at the side of his tautly held jaw. 'And you call that being *rational?* ' he mocked with a decided bite. 'When he allows himself to be convinced by a pair of eloquent eyes and a wistful expression? Hell, I never would have believed it of him! Of course . . .' he suddenly bent his head menacingly nearer, 'when you calculatingly insinuate my personal feelings could be involved and, as a result, feel it could impair *my* judgement as to the corporation's best interest if I let those feelings influence me into accepting you for the position, that could have had some bearing on his decision, I guess!' It was possible to hear his teeth snap together in his fury.

Mallory couldn't control the flush that rose in her cheeks, and found herself suddenly back on the defensive. 'I didn't exactly say that,' she sought to evade uncomfortably.

'No, you were too smart for that! You simply implied it, and allowed his imagination to fill in the supposed details! The result being, I suspect he now sees himself as playing some sort of cupid, thanks to you!' He shook his head savagely and fixed her with a corrosively satirical glare. 'Let's just hope that after having been pleased to make such implications, you find the consequences equally satisfying.'

Her stomach constricted. 'Such as?'

Bren gave a tight, taunting smile. 'Your little ploy has already ensured we shall be in very close contact for the next three months, by virtue of J.B.'s having appointed me as your advisor—and critical appraiser'—that was inserted with relish, she suspected—'instead of your stepfather. As if I haven't other more important matters to be attending to!' His mouth levelled in exasperation.

'Although you do intend to give me a fair trial, at least?' she hazarded anxiously.

'You mean, in the same way you were fair in sneaking down here behind my back, and having my holiday summarily cancelled in the process?' Bren returned in a caustic drawl.

Mallory caught at her lip with pearly teeth. Oh lord, she'd forgotten that. 'Yes—well—I am sorry that happened,' she felt obliged to say. And, raising earnest eyes, 'I just wanted a chance to prove what I could do, that was all!'

'In making things grow?' He flicked a dark brow sarcastically high. 'You could have done that—and more appropriately, I'm thinking—by buying a couple of pot-plants.'

'Oh, don't be so damned patronising!' she immediately condemned stormily. 'You're not the only one with new ideas regarding farming! I've a few of my own, too, you know!'

'Mmm, so I was informed! Such as investigating the possible time and cost-saving factors involved in utilising contract harvesters, for instance. A proposition *I*, coincidentally, just happened to mention a couple of days ago, as I recall!'

'And maybe you were merely echoing my thoughts when you did so!'

'How fortuitous!'

'Yes, wasn't it?' she agreed, facetiously. 'With our minds so attuned you'll have no alternative but to submit a fair report in due course, will you?'

Bren hunched a broad shoulder impassively. 'Except that it always was going to be fair . . . to Banfield's, at any rate.'

'But not to me, is that what you're saying?' Mallory demanded, and was raked with a coolly disdainful gaze for her efforts.

'Well, if you consider it's not, I'm sure you'll have no hesitation in creeping back here for another secret appointment with J.B. in order to make your feelings known and circumvent any assessment I may make!' he charged on a scathing note. Pausing, he bent forward a little, his eyes glinting with the sheen of blue steel. 'But just remember . . . no matter how successful you feel you've been to date, and Joshua Banfield notwithstanding, it's still *me* you'll be working with, and you can take my word for it that I won't be making any allowances, nor do I intend making things easy for you either!'

'So, did I suggest that you should?' she retorted with a gibing defensiveness, doing her best to ignore the consternation his words created. Naturally she hadn't expected him to accept her appointment meekly, but the prospect of a totally hostile Bren Dalton she had to admit was more than a little daunting. 'I merely asked for a chance to prove myself, nothing more.'

'But only if I feel inclined to give you one!' Bren reminded her with an incisive nod. 'And now that you understand that, perhaps we had better return to the party. I wouldn't want J.B. thinking I'm attempting to monopolise your company,' with heavily weighted mockery, 'especially since I'm also under instructions to introduce you to the other members of the corporation present.' He turned to open the door and, with a sardonic gesture that was at odds with his expression, made for her to precede him from the room.

CHAPTER FOUR

BY the time Mallory eventually returned to her own room in the hotel it was after midnight and, kicking off her shoes, she dropped wearily on to the bed. She felt both physically and emotionally drained and, if the truth were known, close to tears. As far as she was concerned the evening had been nothing short of a disaster and she couldn't rememebr when she had last, if ever, felt quite so despondent.

OK, so she could concede that Bren did have grounds for being annoyed. Infuriated, more like, she recollected miserably. She had been somewhat underhand, when all was said and done. Although only because he had so adamantly refused even to consider she might possess other abilities beside those required for modelling, she felt entitled to excuse herself. None the less, had he had to be quite so critical of her *all* evening? She despaired. It seemed nothing she did met with his approval, not even her attempt to relieve him of her obviously rankling presence by spending time in Eric's company. Inexplicably, that had only apppeared to rile him even more.

It didn't exactly make for a promising trial period, Mallory reflected with a dispirited sigh as she curled up with an arm beneath her head as it rested on the pillow. In fact, she wondered if her trip to Melbourne had actually achieved anything, really—except postpone the time when Bren would ensure his decision not to employ her was upheld. As he doubtless meant to do, which somehow made all her hopes and efforts to the contrary seem worthless and futile.

After all, was there any point in continuing when he had evidently already decided what the result was going to be? She might as well give him the satisfaction of a victory now, and save herself all the exertion and frustration involved in trying to achieve the unattainable. The fact that it would also mean surrendering her last chance to remain at Avalon had a tear squeezing beneath her lashes and slowly coursing down her smooth cheek. Suddenly, others were following swiftly as she railed desolately against the one-sidedness of it all. Damn him, why couldn't he at least have been prepared to view the matter with an open mind?

Although sleep eventually claimed her, it was only for an hour or so, Mallory noted from the clock by her bed when her eyes opened drowsily, and then, still only half awake, blinked in confusion on realising she wasn't alone any longer either. Still dressed as she had last seen him, except that he had discarded his jacket and loosened his tie, Bren was squatting on his haunches beside the bed, his regard unfathomable as he surveyed her.

'Do you always leave your hotel-room doors unlocked?' He was the first to speak, in a mixture of sardonic and censuring accents. 'Or were you expecting someone?' A dark brow peaked meaningfully.

Feeling too weary and disconsolate even to alter her position, let alone deny his suggestion, Mallory merely shrugged uncaringly. 'I must have forgotten to lock it when I came in,' she said with a sigh.

Then, in even more lack-lustre tones, 'What are you doing here, anyway?'

For a moment he didn't reply as he continued to scrutinise her closely, and then he unexpectedly touched a finger to her still damp cheek and, exhaling heavily himself, said, 'You've been crying.'

With her wet lashes as extra evidence, there seemed little to be gained in attempting any disclaimer, although she did hastily brush the last traces away. 'Yes—well—at least the sight of me with red and puffy eyes should prove less offensive to you than my presence usually is,' she charged, attempting at least to show some spirit.

To her surprise, Bren smiled at that. A rueful smile admittedly, but so unaccustomed and so disarming that, in spite of her despondent mood, she was more than conscious of the responsive leap in her pulse.

'Except that your eyes don't go red and puffy . . . as I should have guessed!' he remarked with an unexpectedly dry self-mockery. 'They simply darken to a luminous and even more beautiful violet.' He shook his head in what, had it been anyone else, she would have called a defeated movement. 'In any case, no man in his right mind could ever find you offensive to look at, sweetheart, no matter what the circumstances.'

Mallory could only stare at him in confusion. Had she heard him correctly, she wondered, unable fully to credit or understand his seeming change in manner, much less the reason for it. Could it be that, as a result of her tears, he had already deduced she would soon be out of his hair—and his life? Or, the strangely disagreeable thought ensued, was it merely a reflection of the gratification he had been afforded on having escorted Charlene Myers home?

'I think you're confusing me with someone else,' she quipped flatly in consequence. 'And you haven't yet explained why you're here.'

'Neither have you as to why you were crying.' His mouth took on an ironic slant. 'You and Cummings had a falling out, did you?'

He was so wide of the mark that Mallory felt an odd desire to laugh. Not that she could determine just why he would presume she and Eric were close enough to have a falling out. Had Charelene given him the idea, perhaps?

With a deprecating hunch of her shoulder, she disclosed, 'No, it had nothing to do with him.'

In one supple, fluid action, Bren abruptly rose upright, his magnetic blue eyes unwavering as they continued to hold hers. 'So what was it, then?'

Mallory shifted restively at his persistence, and against the feeling of being overwhelmed as he towered over her, his height and muscled form dominating the entire room. 'As if you can't guess!' The words erupted from her involuntarily as she pushed herself up from her pillow at last, only in order to turn her back on him before burying her head in its softness again. 'Why can't you just be satisfied with having won, and leave me alone!' Tears started to prick the back of her eyes once more.

'I might . . . if I knew what in blazes you were talking about!' Bren grated roughly, his grip no less forceful when he bent to rest one knee on the side of the bed and his hand dragged her back to face him again. 'Now . . . won *what* might I ask?'

Angrily dashing a hand across her eyes, Mallory glared up at him rancorously. 'I've decided against becoming the manager at Avalon, after all!' she threw back at him on a bitter note.

'Oh, have you!' Much to her astonishment, instead of appeasing him, her revelation seemed to infuriate him even more. 'The novelty worn off already, has it? And faster than even I anticipated, too!' he jeered contemptuously. 'Or is this simply another attempt to create trouble for me—due to my opposition to the idea—by making it appear as if you've been harassed into changing your mind?'

'No!' she protested wrathfully, sitting up quickly now. 'It never was my intention to cause you any trouble . . . as I've already told you! And what's more, I fail to see why anyone should think I had been bullied into changing my mind either!' Not that her decision had been altogether willingly made, just the same, of course!

'Because in view of its not being realised by anyone else that it was purely on impulse—a suddenly and briefly appealing whim of the moment!—that you decided to apply for the position in the first place, then what other construction could be placed on it?' Bren rasped, in a voice strongly laced with sarcasm. 'After all, *you* were the one to imply that our relationship was somewhat more personal than it actually was . . . remember?' He eyed her caustically. 'So what would be more likely than that I now use that—umm—closeness, to prevail upon you to change your mind, because due to my supposedly impaired judgement, I've been set against employing you from the very beginning!'

Although Mallory averted her gaze guiltily, she still didn't feel inclined to accept all the blame. When all was said and done, her use of that prevarication had also been on his behalf; in an effort to *prevent* causing him any trouble!

'Well, if you hadn't been so unreasonable . . .!' she excused herself. But on recalling his prior denigrations, she continued in a less conciliatory vein, 'Moreover, you can cut out all those snide and derogatory comments, too, regarding the novelty having worn off, because nothing could be further from the truth, if you must know! I really did want to make a go of it—I still do—only you've put paid to that!' She took a jagged breath and cast him a speaking glance. 'In fact, come to think of it, since it is because of you that I've changed my mind, maybe it would be no more than you deserve if you did have some explaining to do!'

Bren uttered a derisive snort. 'So it's all my fault now, is it! Well, that's as handy an excuse as any, I guess!'

'Except that I don't happen to need an excuse when I already now what the result will be of any trial I'm likely to receive from you! An unequivocal thumbs-down!'

'In other words, you're admitting the truth of what I've maintained all along, hmm? That you're just not capable of holding such a position!'

Mallory bristled. 'No, that isn't it at all!' she denied hotly. 'And stop trying to twist my words, Bren Dalton! You seem to forget that you've already told me that your report isn't going to favour me!' She looked away, chewing at her lip moodily. 'So what's the point in my even starting the job when I know it will all be for nothing?'

Watching her, Bren ran a hand around the back of his neck irritably, and then bent to tilt her face up to his as he seated himself on the side of the bed. 'And just how long do you reckon I'd last in *my* position if the reports I submitted were formulated that arbitrarily, huh?' he quizzed in a half-exasperated, half-ironic drawl. 'I merely said I wouldn't be making any allowances or making things easy for you, that's all.' He paused, his lips twitching lazily. 'And if I remember correctly, you said you hadn't suggested I should.'

Mallory shook free of his touch vexedly, the movement disposing of the already loosened bow that had been securing her hair, so that now the long silvery strands fell against her shoulders like a shimmering curtain. 'You also said you were only going to be fair to Banfield's!' she accused.

'Well, they are my main concern. But not that that necessarily precludes any fairness being afforded you, in any event. It simply means I put their interests first. Which is as it should be, don't you think? Or were you mistakenly thinking that your previous smiles and honeyed manner should have been sufficient to have me switching my allegiance?' The sweep of his mouth was cynically mocking.

'No!' she refuted with some asperity, her violet eyes darkening. Heavens, he really did distrust her! Or was it just the whole female species! 'I smile because it comes naturally—you should try it some time!—and, for your information, my manner is not *honeyed!*' The word had connotations of insincerity she found distinctly distasteful. Simultaneously, however, his other words held implications that were of greater concern to her, and her aggrieved feelings swiftly became submerged beneath ones of faintly rising hope as she eyed him diffidently. 'But—do you mean that you really are . . . willing to give me a chance? That you haven't already decided what the result is going to be?'

For a moment their glances held, and then Bren expelled a resigned breath, his mouth curving obliquely. 'I don't have much choice, do I?'

He was meaning because of the position she had put him in, Mallory deduced, and bit at her lip regretfully. 'I'm sorry . . . but you don't realise how much this means to me!' she tried to impress on him.

'Although God only knows why!' Bren retorted, shaking his head incredulously, and surprising her with the sudden rough tautness in his voice. 'For crying out loud, can't you see you're just not suited to the work . . . to the rigours of the land! You know as well as I do that, even as manager, you'll still be doing physical work, and . . .' he abruptly caught hold of one of her hands, turning it palm uppermost, 'how do you think these are going to stand up to it, for a start? They're as soft and smooth as silk!' Pausing, he gave another shake of his head. 'And should be,' came the surprising assertion in a deeper tone. 'Not like that!' With an expressive twist to his lips, he held one of his own work-hardened hands next to hers for comparison.

That consideration for her might have formed part of his opposition, Mallory had never suspected, and she half smiled deprecatingly. 'I can always wear gloves.'

This reply merely earned a sardonic look before he proposed in a similarly satirical fashion, 'You have an equally simplistic, and improbable, solution for ensuring you remain in control of the men on the property, too, I suppose?'

A faint frown made an appearance between her arched brows. Now what was he getting at? 'Since I've always got along very well with Dick Crowley and Max Salter in the past, I don't expect any problems in that regard,' she put forward with a shrug.

'Except that, with two other properties being added to the holding, they won't be the only men on the place any more! There will be a number of others as well, and unmarried ones at that, most likely!' Bren's voice tightenened fractionally.

Implying, they may not be so ready to accept a female in the role of manager? 'I—well—I can't see why you should think that will automatically present problems. I'm not the type to become officious and start throwing my weight around, if that's what you mean.' A reassuring thought came to her rescue. 'Nor, might I add, did Joshua Banfield apparently foresee any such difficulties either.'

'Probably because Joshua Banfield has no experience whatever of working on a property in the bush. I have!' The last was delivered with succinct meaning. 'And although the Wimmera may not be the rough-and-ready outback, when you have a number of unattached males working in reasonable isolation, there's still the possibility the result may not necessarily be so different on occasion. They work hard, they play hard . . . and they drink hard! So, tell me, what are you going to do if one of them returns from town on Saturday night, tanked to the eyeballs, and decides to get a bit stroppy with the boss-lady . . . who, as it so happens, isn't precisely the worst-looking bird around?'

Mallory couldn't restrain the wry curve that caught at her lips. Not the worst-looking bird around? Until a couple of weeks ago she had been known for her ability to turn heads; for being the face everyone just *had* to have in their magazines!

'All that flattery will go to my head if you're not careful!' she quipped. But on noting his darkening expression, she hurried on to declare in a less glib manner, 'While as for the other . . . well, *if* it ever became necessary, I guess I could, as a last resort, always yell for help from Dick, or—or anyone else who happened to be around.'

'Only if there were someone else around, of course!'

Grimacing, Mallory angled her head higher. 'I'm not totally helpless, you know, Bren! I've managed to look after myself quite successfully for some years now . . . and that includes repulsing any unwanted attentions from the opposite sex!'

He dipped his head in acknowledgement—mockingly, she suspected. 'That's heartening news! At least I won't have the added responsibility now of worrying that you can't extricate yourself if some feller takes it into his head to start something like this!' Without warning his hand descended on to her shoulders and she was pulled close against his muscular form, and kept there by an arm encircling her back, leaving the other hand free to ensnare her chin and tilt it upwards. 'Perhaps you would care to demonstrate just how you would go about it?' His sable-lashed eyes filled with sardonic light.

Already shaken by the unbelievable awareness of him that was assailing her—and deducing any struggle she put up would be ineffectual—Mallory chose to respond with words instead of actions, doing her utmost to conceal her suddenly heightened feelings beneath a composed exterior.

'In this instance, there's no need,' she claimed with a hopefully impassive shrug. 'After all, we

both know exactly how you feel about me, so I've
hardly any worries where you're concerned, have I?'
She ventured to flash him a faintly chafing glance of
her own.

'Haven't you?' Bren countered in abruptly
shortening accents, his hands pushing into her hair
and cupping her head between them. 'I doubt
there's a man alive who could remain unresponsive
to you for very long . . . and I guess I'm no
exception!' The seemingly reluctant admission was
delivered in an almost self-mocking fashion as his
mouth closed determinedly over hers.

At the initial unanticipated contact, Mallory
stiffened. She really hadn't believed he intended
going further than proving his own previous point,
but since he had, she fully expected his kiss to be of
the punishing variety rather than anything else. And
so he had originally meant it to be, too, she
surmised, when his lips began moving against hers
forcefully. Only briefly, then a subtle change
occurred. Instead of overpowering, they gradually
became persuasive, seeking a response and not
suppressing one, and disconcertingly arousing
emotions she found impossible to control.

Now she knew the answer to the question that had
intrigued her at their first meeting regarding which
of those traits prevailed that she had seen expressed
in his mouth. It seemed the sensuousness and
generosity came to the fore in his lovemaking, and
she responded to their tantalising stimulation
compulsively.

With her lips parting beneath the seductive caress
of his, Bren traced the inside of their soft contours
stirringly with the tip of his tongue before making a
deeper, more intimate exploration of the sweet

recesses of her mouth, and Mallory's breathing began to quicken. Running her hands experimentally across his powerful chest, she savoured the feel of the hard muscles beneath his shirt, then linked her fingers tightly at the back of his neck as a coil of heat, of unmistakable desire, suddenly began to burn in the pit of her stomach. Somewhere, her earlier interest in him had intensified to definite attraction, she realised.

'Yes—well . . . ' Bren's voice sounded husky when he at last raised his head and released her. Contemplatively, he continued to regard her from beneath half narrowed lids, although the expression in his magnetic blue eyes was impossible to define. 'That kind of reaction certainly could set any would-be Romeo back on his heels . . . even if not exactly deter him,' he claimed in an expressive drawl.

The inherent irony in his tone had Mallory colouring self-consciously. 'Including you?' she dared to enquire in defence, albeit a touch throatily.

For a time his gaze remained fixed speculatively on hers, and then he rose to his feet to stand with his hands resting on lean hips, and shook his head, decisively. 'Save that I don't happen to fit into that category'

Nor was it quite what she had been meaning—as she had a sneaking suspicion he was aware—but she didn't pursue it. In lieu, she merely hunched a slender shoulder and murmured, 'Although, as I recall, you haven't as yet said exactly what brought you to my room at this hour.'

Surprisingly, a lazy smile took possession of his mouth in response, and had her breath constricting in her throat as a result. 'Only to advise you not to make any arrangements for returning to Avalon today, if that was your intention.' He paused. 'And only then, of course, provided you are still interested in taking on the role of manager.' He arched a dark brow provokingly.

'Yes, of course I am!' Mallory confirmed rapidly, and testily in the face of that taunting look. It had only been because of him that she had had doubts in the first place! 'But why shouldn't I return home today? I had planned to.'

Bren executed an unconcerned gesture. 'Then I'm afraid you'll just have to alter those plans, because it's been—suggested,' from the faint pause, Mallory ruefully suspected it had to be more in the nature of a directive to which he had to comply, 'I take you to head office in the morning . . . in order to fill in the relevant personnel forms so that you can be listed officially as a member of Banfield's staff.' He took an audible breath. 'You are also invited to the party J.B.'s giving at his home tomorrow night.'

Mallory's eyes widened in astonishment. 'But why would he invite me to a party at his home?'

'Probably because all his senior staff are invited, and *someone*,' acidly stressed, 'gave him the impression that you were somewhat—umm—involved, with one of them!' she was advised in acrimoniously mocking tones.

'Oh!' She dropped her gaze discomfitedly. 'Well, you could always give my excuses and say . . .'

'And anything in that line has already been vetoed!' Bren cut in on a dismissive note. 'You are expected!'

'I—well—I know it's a terrible cliché, but I honestly don't have anything to wear,' Mallory suddenly recalled with a grimace. 'This is the only suitable dress I brought with me,' indicating the chiffon she was still clothed in, 'but I can't wear it tomorrow as well.'

'Then I guess you'll just have to find some other way of solving the problem, won't you? Far be it from me to keep reminding you, but . . . you did create it!'

'Thanks!' Mallory sent him a graphic look as she mentally began sorting through her options. She could buy one, of course, but she really didn't want to. Not when she already owned enough to fill a wardrobe, and her future chances of wearing all of those even were obviously going to be limited. Perhaps she could borrow one from Bronwyn, another model with whom she had previously shared an apartment, she mused. They were of much the same size, and they had certainly borrowed each other's clothes on many occasions when they were first starting out. Yes, that was the best idea, she decided. She would give Bronwyn a call early in the morning to ensure she was amenable, and then visit her some time later in the day once her own dealings with Bren were concluded. 'So how long is our business later this morning likely to take?' she now asked of him with this thought in mind.

'Not very long, hopefully. Although you've succeeded in reducing it considerably, I still would like *some* time in which to conduct my private affairs!' His return was larded with pungent sarcasm, and a suspected implication that had Mallory feeling peculiarly out of sorts. He had meant with regard to his relationship with Charlene Myers, she supposed.

'Well, don't blame me!' she flared tartly in consequence. 'I didn't ask to be constantly in your company either!'

'No, you just set the wheels in motion, that's all!' Bren retorted, lips twisting expressively. He started for the door with a tense stride. 'So just make sure you're ready to leave at eight . . . right? I have an intense dislike for unpunctuality in members of my staff!'

Mallory lifted her chin higher. 'That's good, because I dislike it in anyone!' she fired back, eyeing him significantly. 'So I don't expect you to keep me waiting either!'

'I won't!' He nodded in emphasis before taking his departure.

With his exit, Mallory's emotions immediately cooled, and she pulled a wry face. Her flashes of fieriness rarely lasted long, and truth to tell, she owned with a rueful smile, she had discovered that kissing him was far more pleasurable than fighting with him.

Despite the few hours of sleep left to her, Mallory was still dressed and waiting in the hotel foyer when Bren arrived later that morning. And right on the stroke of eight, she noted.

She was wearing the same lemon-coloured slacks and high-heeled sandals she had worn for her journey the day before, but on this occasion teamed with a cotton top patterned in bright, fruit-salad colours, and a chunky necklace of peach-toned coral. Her hair she had caught back in a single, thick plait, with only a wispy fringe to grace her smooth forehead, but regardless of its casualness, and that of her attire, there still wasn't a person in the vicinity who wasn't aware of her; who hadn't turned to look at her at least a second time. She simply had that innate style, not to mention the endowment of superb features and form, that made her stand out wherever she went, and although Mallory had become reconciled to it—indeed, had profited substantially from it—it soon became evident that it affected Bren quite differently.

'Yes, well, if you feel you've put on enough of a show, and you can bear to drag yourself away from your admirers,' as another two male guests surveyed her with open appreciation on passing them, 'do you think we might get going now?' he queried with biting savagery only minutes after she had crossed the floor to meet him. 'Since I've been forced to concentrate so much of my time on Avalon, there are a great many matters requiring my attention today!'

Hurt both by his accusation and by the fact that he apparently was still as riled as he had been when he left the hotel earlier, Mallory merely gave a toss of her head and began walking swiftly—stalking would have been a better word—towards the front doors. Only when they were seated in his vehicle—a dark green Fairlane this time, she noticed with a slight frown—did she give vent to her feelings.

'I can't help the looks I was born with, Bren! Any more than anyone can!' she protested, her eyes shaded with unknowing reproach. 'The only reason I was waiting for you in the foyer was I thought it might save you some time . . . not because of any desire to attract attention! It might surprise you to learn that sometimes all that staring can be quite embarrassing, and nor do I particularly enjoy being ogled by lecherous males! But unless you're suggesting I should go around in sackcloth and ashes, and with a hood over my head, there's not

much I can do about it!' To her surprise, and
disquiet, she suddenly felt the salt of tears in her eyes
and turned away quickly to stare out of the window.

Having been about to draw out into the traffic,
Bren now brought the car to a halt again. 'OK—I'm
sorry,' he apologised roughly, heavily. 'I shouldn't
have said what I did. It wasn't fair.' Leaning across,
he brought her face back to his, his mouth assuming
a rueful tilt as he scanned her aggrieved features
intently. 'You're right, you *can't* help being blessed
with a beauty that defies description.' He drew a
finger along her delicate jawline, an unexpectedly
teasing note entering his voice as he drawled, 'Or
would that be construed as lechery on my part?'

Mallory bent her head. It was strange, but she
wanted to appear beautiful to him, wanted *him* to be
so aware of her that he looked twice. 'How can you
be lecherous about someone you don't even like?'
she countered huskily with a deprecating shrug.

'I thought we'd gone through all that last night,'
he returned on a dry note. 'Of all the emotions you
arouse, sweetheart, I can assure you dislike isn't
among them.' Then as if regretting having revealed
so much, he swung back to set the car in motion
once more with tautly controlled movements. 'It's
your general mode of operation that I find
objectionable.'

And particularly her most recent effort, she
surmised, sighing, and judiciously decided not to
reply. That would only serve to keep the matter in
his mind longer. Instead, she directed her attention
to the buildings they were passing, noting the
changes, even in the few short years she had been
away, and remembering those times when she, too,
had been part of the same busy scene.

It didn't take long for them to reach the Banfield building, but as they left the Fairlane in the underground parking area and made for the lift Mallory once again regarded the dark green vehicle with a frown.

'Is that your own car?' she asked curiously as the doors of the lift closed behind them.

He shrugged. 'Well, company-provided for my use. Why?'

She spread one hand indecisively. 'I just expected you still to be using the four-wheel-drive you had at Avalon, I guess.'

'That would have been a little difficult since it's in Nyandra.'

Still in Nyandra? Her frown returned in full force. 'Then how . . .?'

'I flew down . . . in the company plane I used to get there,' Bren supplied in faintly mocking tones, correctly interpreting the cause of her bewilderment. 'The Range Rover is merely rented and was delivered to the airstrip prior to my arrival. I don't have the time to waste spending unnecessarily long hours on the road whenever I visit the corporation's holdings.' He paused, significantly. 'That is, I didn't, until someone's machinations engendered the decision to have me paying close attention to one particular property during the next few months!'

Mallory swallowed and caught at her lip with even white teeth. Apparently this hadn't been the most auspicious topic she could have raised either. But at least now she understood how he had managed to arrive in Melbourne so swiftly the preivous day, something that had puzzled her from the time he had made his appearance. And thereby almost succeeded in beating her to see Joshua Banfield, she reflected

with another gulp. The possible consequences of
that could have been demoralising, and thwarting,
in the extreme.

At that moment the lift reached their floor, and as
the doors slid open and they crossed the carpeted
hallway to the gold-lettered, plate-glass doors
opposite, Mallory was thankful for the opportunity it
provided to steer the conversation in another
direction.

'Is this where you work when you're in
Melbourne?' she asked after Bren had unlocked the
doors and they entered the spacious and stylishly
furnished reception area. Then she promptly gave a
gasp of dismay, her eyes widening, on thinking that
might not have been the most prudent question to
ask either at the present time.

Recognising her look once again, however, Bren
shook his head wryly. 'Don't worry, anything that
keeps me in the bush I find quite acceptable,' he
owned.

Relieved, Mallory smiled widely in understanding, and momentarily Bren didn't move, but
continued looking at her, his ebony-lashed blue gaze
disturbingly appraising as it lingered on her
beguiling mouth, so that she was propelled into
moistening its soft contours with the tip of her
tongue to overcome its abrupt feeling of dryness.

The movement seemed to galvanise Bren into
action and, turning sharply, he started for one of the
office-lined passageways that led from the area.
'This way,' he advised brusquely, and recovering
some of her composure, Mallory followed him
obediently.

He turned in at the second doorway, but on doing
the same Mallory noticed that the name on the door

wasn't his. 'This isn't your office,' she stated rather
than asked as a result, and more as a means of
alleviating the charged astomphere than anything
else.

'No, it's Sid Dyson's—the personnel manager.
You met him last night,' Bren replied absently,
waving her to a chair in front of the leather-topped
desk where he had already taken a seat and was
searching through its drawers.

Disregarding the chair, Mallory nodded as she
moved to the windows instead to look out over the
city, and mentally pictured the somewhat rotund,
chubby-cheeked man with the cherubic countenance
who had immediately put her at her ease the
previous evening. A very beneficial characteristic in
a personnel manager, she guessed.

'Ah, here it is!' Bren's satisfied exclamation
caught her attention again as he extracted a pad of
forms from a lower drawer. Then picking up a pen,
he eyed her enquiringly. 'Now—full name . . .?'

While providing it—and all the other relevant
particulars, both personal and otherwise, that were
requested—Mallory wandered about the office
desultorily, taking in the quality fixtures and
fittings, the quietly plush furnishings, and the up-to-
the-minute equipment. Along one wall there was an
open door that gave access to another, smaller office.
Not quite so elegantly appointed, but no less
attractively designed for all that; the fittings therein,
including the video terminal and computer keyboard
resting on the tubular steel-framed desk, giving rise
to the presumption that it was the domain of Sid
Dyson's secretary.

This speculation was shortly confirmed by Bren's
proposing, 'You'll probably find a job description

sheet in the filing-cabinet just inside the doorway there, if you'd care to look for it.' He retrieved a key from a locked drawer of the desk he was utilising and held it out to her. 'You'll need this, though.'

Accepting it, Mallory headed into the next room, from where she was able to continue supplying the answers to his questions as she set about opening the cabinet and seeking the appropriate paperwork. A job description could be extremely handy, especially in her circumstances, she decided.

One glance at the labels on the files filling the top drawer was sufficient to have her realising that they were the corporation's private files on their personnel—just like the one Bren was now completing concerning her—but on the point of closing the drawer again a sudden, ungovernable idea took hold of her, and she began flicking through the individual folders instead until she came to the one that had inspired her interest. If it was acceptable for Bren to know all her personal details, why shoudn't she also discover what she could about him? she attempted to assuage her feelings of guilt as she hurriedly, furtively, started to scan the detailed pages.

So Bren wasn't a shortened version of his name, after all, as she had suspected. And, as her stepfather had said, he had indeed originally come from New South Wales. Although whether the outback, as Ward had also mentioned, she couldn't decide. Lord, who knew where Marramaronga Flat might be? She had never heard of it! Hmm, that was strange, though, she frowned on passing to the next entry. The initial notation regarding his date of birth had, presumably at some latter time judging by the difference in handwriting, been reduced by three

years. Now why would that have been? she puzzled,
although without the time for any lengthy
deliberation, reluctantly she had to put it to one side
as she moved on.

Well, he had certainly worked in outback New
South, she discoverd next. On a property that, like
Avalon, had evidently also been taken over by
Banfield's. And then hadn't his promotion been
rapid! Within the year, made manager of the very
same property, and at only eighteen, as she recalled
Duncan mentioning; transferred two years later to
take charge of another property, in South Australia
this time, and then again to another · one in
Queensland. From there he had risen to manager of
all the coporation's eastern States' pastoral
enterprises; and then, four years ago, he had been
made Field Manager of their whole rural division.
And every one of those promotions recommended by
none other than Joshua Banfield himself . . .
together with a salary commensurate with that
man's faith in his ability! she suddenly realised with
an embarrassed gulp on inadvertently viewing the
amounts. Discovery of Bren's actual wage hadn't
been her intent.

'The money meets with your approval?' Bren's
sardonically voiced query had Mallory starting, and
reddening helplessly as she quickly thrust the folder
back into the cabinet. Had he somehow seen her
reading his file?

'H-how do you mean?' she parried faintly,
holding her breath.

'How do you think I mean?' A partly impatient,
partly satirical edge make an appearance in his tone.
'Your salary, naturally! I understood J.B. had
discussed it with you.'

'Oh, that!' In a relieved rush she released the breath she had been holding, and felt sufficiently reassured to move fully into sight in the doorway to give an off-hand shrug. 'If that't the going rate, it seems acceptable,' she allowed.

'Not too much of a come-down for you?' mockingly.

Well, it was certainly that, Mallory ruefully had to concede. Although she doubted that disclosing it wasn't unusual for her to make as much in only a couple of weeks while modelling was likely to help her cause. In any event, since she had given up that profession, she was evidently going to have to re-accustom herself to a reduced income from now on anyway.

'No, not when it's compensated for by work-satisfaction,' she returned levelly.

An expressive curve moulded Bren's mouth. 'Yeah, well, let's just hope it provides Banfield's with equal satisfaction.' He paused, his metallic blue eyes challenging when she gave a gibing grimace in response. 'Something that appears highly unlikely if, as it seems, you aren't even capable of locating the job description sheets.'

Mallory's grimace turned into a sparkling glare.

'Only because I wasn't aware it was a matter of dire urgency!' she retorted, and flounced back to the filing-cabinet to drag open the second drawer.

When that proved to contain only more personnel files, she closed it again and moved down to the next. Luckily, this turned out to be more rewarding, and, swiftly passing over those sheets marked for other divisions within the corporation, she was soon successful in finding one that applied to her own position.

'I trust that was suitably efficient?' she allowed herself the pleasure of enquiring facetiously on returning to the main office.

Bren held her gaze steadily. 'Provided you also remembered to lock the filing-cabinet again, of course.'

Smiling triumphantly, Mallory held the key aloft with a flourish before placing it on the desk in front of him. 'Of course,' she copied on a chaffing note.

Except for one last explicit glance, and a cynical twist to his lips, Bren didn't respond. He merely returned his attention to his writing, and left Mallory to cool her heels as best she could until he at last condescended to tell her that it was time they were leaving, and he drove her back to the hotel.

CHAPTER FIVE

AS she had arranged earlier in the day, Mallory visited her friend Bronwyn during the afternoon. The outcome of the pleasantly casual and humorously reminiscing interlude was the loan of a suitable creation to wear to Joshua Banfield's party, and a relaxed frame of mind as Mallory made ready later that evening.

The dress she had borrowed was of slinky silk in tones of lilac and aqua. Slim-fitting from its shoestring-strap top to just below the hips, it then flared into a whirl of pleats that left a length of tanned and shapely leg on display. Her accessories, also lent by Bronwyn, were a pair of lilac, strappy high-heeled sandals and matching evening purse; her jewellery a three-strand pearl choker, set with a square-cut amethyst that she mated with her own drop earrings which she had worn the night before.

Now, with her make-up applied—and as, always, only enough to heighten her features, not bury them—Mallory piled her hair artfully on top of her head, securing it with a couple of pearl-decorated combs, and prepared to wait for Bren's arrival. Tonight she very definitely would not be making the effort to save him time by waiting for him in the lobby, she decided wryly;

And perhaps it was just as well, she went on to speculate a short time later on opening the door to him, because she simply wasn't prepared for the way his physical presence seemed to assualt her senses. She didn't know whether it was because he looked just so attractive—his dark grey suit was impeccably cut and became him so well—or because of the lazily sensuous look that filtered into his incredibly blue eyes on his initial inspection of her, but abruptly she was very much aware of her pulse pounding erratically and her legs feeling distinctly weak.

'Well, no guesses as to who's going to be the centre of attention tonight, hmm?' Bren declared in a dry drawl. His mouth sloped crookedly. 'You really are an absolute stunner, aren't you, sweetheart?'

Mallory swallowed. 'You don't look so unpleasing yourself,' she pushed out banteringly, although how she managed it she had no idea.

He tilted his head in a mocking acknowledgment. 'Then let's hope it helps to remind you that we are supposed to spend at least some time together this evening.'

Mallory's eyes flickered. She had anticipated their spending most of their time together, but apparently he had other ideas. Breathing deeply in an effort to overcome the heavy feeling that suddenly seemed to have lodged in her chest, she forced a careless smile on to her lips.

'How could I possibly forget? That was the main reason I was invited, wasn't it?' Without waiting for an answer, she picked up her purse and turned for the door.

Bren followed in silence, his expression inscrutable. In fact, neither of them spoke again as they journeyed down in the lift, nor as they made their way out of the city along Toorak Road. Mallory was too engrossed in recovering her earlier feeling of wellbeing to attempt to convince herself she didn't care if he spent any time with her or not. While as for Bren . . . well, she supposed he was simply trying to reconcile himself with having been compelled to escort her at all.

When they finally turned in through the tall, wrought-iron gates that gave access to the curving gravel driveway leading to the fountain-adorned forecourt of Joshua Banfield's double-storey, light-emblazoned, and already gaily thronged mansion, Mallory couldn't control the involuntary sigh that escaped her. It was all so similar to innumerable other parties she had attended during the last few years.

'I had thought that being employed on a property would exempt me from all this,' she found herself disclosing ruefully, spontaneously.

Squeezing into a parking-space between a Rolls and a Mercedes, Bren regarded her consideringly for a moment, and then his lips levelled. 'Maybe you should have thought of that before implying there was some connection between us.' He continued almost immediately as he began opening his door. 'Although I'm sure having Eric and Duncan, and doubtless many others dancing attendance upon you will soon have you feeling in your element once more!'

Mallory pressed her lips together, and releasing her seat-belt with a snap, alighted quickly. 'Implying that all it requires to keep me happy is some flattery and being the centre of attention, is that it?' she demanded, sending him a nettled glare across the bonnet of the car. 'Well, much as it may surprise you, Bren Dalton, I just don't happen to be that shallow!'

He arched an eloquent brow. 'Yet it was part and parcel of the life-style you willingly pursued, and evidently enjoyed, for the last three years or more.'

'But not the reason for my having done so!'

'Then what was?'

Resentment had her blurting out what she had never divugled to anyone before. 'If you must know it was the only means available to earn enough money to enable me to buy Avalon! I love that place and I wanted to surprise Ward with it!' She swallowed. 'But Banfield's put an end to that, and when Ward resigned and—and . . . ' Breaking off, she bit down hard on her lip to halt its betraying trembling. 'And damn you for always being so disparaging and cynical! I *was* in a good mood until you arrived!'

Bren looked away, raking a hand roughly through his hair, but when he looked back again it was with an entirely unexpected tilt catching at his mouth. 'Although not because you were looking forward to tonight's grand affair, presumably,' he hazarded in the driest of tones.

Disconcertingly caught unawares, Mallory shook her head jerkily. Something in his manner emboldened her to ask in a soft voice, 'Were you?'

The even more wryly expressive shaping of his mouth was answer enough, and all at once her lips began to curve irrepressibly in response, a warm feeling inside suddenly taking hold of her. She felt as if they shared something, as if for once he had actually allowed her to get a little closer to him, and she savoured the sensation pleasurably.

'Nevertheless, since we are required to attend . . .' Bren drawled philosophically, holding out an inviting hand towards her.

Moving around the vehicle to join him, Mallory half smiled in resignation. 'We may as well get it over and done with as soon as possible.' Then, venturing to cast him a twinkling glance from the cover of her long, curling lashes, she proposed conspiratorially, 'You don't suppose we could leave early, do you?'

Abruptly, Bren grinned, and after having previously recommended that he should smile more often, Mallory now wondered if maybe it was just as well he didn't, for there was an irresistible quality about him when he did so that she found quite devastating.

'In view of the fact that it isn't unkown for J.B.'s parties to include breakfast the following morning, that's usually a foregone conclusion where I'm concerned,' he told her on a whimical note as they started for the brightly-lit entrance of the impressive residence. 'For someone raised in the outback, who still spends most of his time in the bush, I'm afraid I find the meaningless patter that passes for conversation at these purely social affairs decidedly less than gripping.' Pausing, he brought their movements to a stop beside the fountain where coloured lights changed the water to every shade of the rainbow, his gaze assuming a probing aspect as it came to rest on her quizzically upturned features. 'And talking of the bush . . . was that the truth about your wanting to buy Avalon?'

Disappointed by both his question and the fact that he seemed to have brought their moment of rapport to an end, her eyes clouded with regret. 'I don't lie, Bren,' she stated reproachfully.

'Although you're not averse to being misleading when it suits you.'

Would he never let her forget that? 'But not this time! Couldn't you tell the difference?' Her voice turned husky with wistfulness.

He shook his head, but whether in rejection or uncertainty she couldn't be sure. 'Then why didn't you ever mention anything about it before?'

Mallory sighed. 'What was the point? Could it—would it—have altered anything?'

He shrugged. 'Except that love of the land is a sentiment I can appreciate.'

'But not love of the other kind?' The words tumbled out before she could even censor the thought that spawned them.

Bren's expression hardened. 'If you're meaning, between two people, then no, I've no time for the sham and mockery of that kind of so-called love,' he conceded with a contemptuous inflection. 'Just the mere word has been mouthed so often, made so cheap and sordid, that it doesn't mean a thing any more!'

Mallory bent her head, chewing at her lip, and regretting her impetuous remark more than ever. She was hardly likely to regain that feeing of accord between them by asking such questions, and particularly not when she had already had a fair suspicion of what his answer would be! Lord, hadn't she previously deduced that women, or at least a woman, had somehow given him cause to think less than highly of her sex? Swallowing, she sought to recover lost ground by reverting to their original topic, which was also important to her.

'Although you do now believe I was telling the truth about wanting to buy Avalon?' she asked anxiously. 'I mean, I even mentioned last night that you didn't realise how much it meant to me.'

'So you did,' he agreed on an audibly released breath.

Whether he meant to add anything Mallory was frustrated in discovering, for just then a sleek Porsche swung into a parking-space a short distance away and Duncan Amery and his effervescent redhead wife Renata alighted.

'Mallory! How lovely to see you again! Duncan told me you might be here tonight!' Renata was the first to speak as she crossed the intervening space and gave the younger girl an affectionate kiss on the cheek. Then, with a mischievous glance upwards, 'And Bren—my favourite hunk—as usual it's good to see you again, too! You know, it's unfair of you to deprive us of your company so often at these gatherings.' She wagged a mock-censuring finger at him.

Bren's lips twitched wryly. 'When business calls . . .' he excused himself with an indolent lifting of his shoulders. 'In any case, this is the second I've attended in as many nights.'

'Mmm, but I couldn't make it to last night's and,' a bubbling laugh sprang forth, 'at a guess I'd say you weren't precisely reconciled to the fact either, judging by your dour demeanour when you arrived.'

'Unless that was for a different reason entirely,' put in Duncan now on a dry note. He slanted an expressive brow as he looked from Bren to Mallory and back again. 'You two wouldn't still be at loggerheads, would you?'

'At loggerheads—two of my favourite people? What on earth for?'

It was obvious from Renata's immediate expostulation that her husband hadn't filled her in with all the details regarding Mallory's return to

Melbourne—for which the younger girl was extremely grateful—but whether Bren was inclined to be as restrained she couldn't be certain, and in consequence the glance she cast in his direction was both apprehensive and unkowingly pleading.

Momentarily, violet eyes locked with cobalt blue, and then Bren gave an imperceptible almost disbelieving, shake of his head, his shapely mouth curving obliquely, and returned his attention to Duncan.

'No, we were merely setting the record straight,' he imparted in wry tones, giving Mallory cause to expel the breath she had been unconsciously holding in a rush of relief and happiness. Not only because he had seen fit not to make any discomfiting disclosures, but also due to the implication that he had accepted her earlier words as the truth.

'There! I knew you had to be wrong!' The look Renata now bestowed on her husband was happily complacent. 'Why, just the idea of Bren—with his connoisseur's taste where women are concerned,' a sparkling glance of teasing raillery was directed at the man in question, 'actually being in conflict with someone like our lovely Mallory, is too unbelievable even to contemplate!' Pausing, she linked an arm with each of them. 'And now that's settled, shall we join the evening's festivities?' She began urging them towards the house.

Acquiescing, and with Duncan keeping pace alongside Mallory, the four of them made their way inside the imposing residence where they were greeted warmly by Joshua Banfield, together with his gracious and elegantly attired wife. For a few minutes they remained in conversation with the older couple, and while they did so Mallory took the

opportunity surreptitiously to view her surroundings.

From the spacious marble-floored entrance
hall—complete with its ornately carved staircase
leading to the upper floor, its magnificent
chandelier, and its miniature replica of the fountain
in the forecourt—to the even more extensive room
beyond the wide connecting archway, with its
sumptuous furnishings and decorations, the whole
impression was one of undeniable style—and
wealth. An impression also created by the obviously
expensive and often elaborate apparel of those quests
already present, Mallory noted as she watched the
white-jacketed waiters move smoothly among them
with their trays of champagne and exotically
coloured cocktails. She didn't doubt that everyone
who was anyone in the city was here tonight.

'Well, what do you think of it?' enquired Bren in
a murmured aside on their finally leaving the
Banfields and moving further into the room where
they were promptly offered flutes of bubbling
champagne from an attentive waiter.

Taking a sip from her glass, Mallory looked about
her again, at the plump, white leather couches and
deep-cushioned armchairs, the low glass-topped
tables with their aesthetic arrangements of flowers,
the wide expanse of thick-piled carpet, and
extravagant Christmas decorations, even the string
quartet who were providing the subdued and sedate
background music.

'It's superb, of course,' she owned at length with
a faint raising of one honey-tinted shoulder. A
wayward tilt caught at her lips and she chanced a
laughing glance upwards. 'But it's not exactly
homely, is it?'

'Uh-uh!' There was something in his laconically drawled agreement, or maybe it was some indefinable expression in his eyes, that made her feel as if they hadn't altogether lost that earlier, brief affinity as she had believed, after all, and it had her senses responding spontaneously. 'Although, to be honest, I don't think they do much of their living in these rooms either,' Bren evidently felt obliged to add. 'As I've seen when I've visited on less formal occasions, there are other areas with a far more personal feel to them.'

Mallory scanned the length of the high ceiling with an explicit gaze. 'Lots of them I shouldn't wonder!' she quipped drily. 'The place is huge!'

'Mmm, it's no bough shed, that's for certain!' he conceded in the same wry manner. 'But then, it's not my idea of . . . '

'There you are, darling!' He was suddenly interrupted by Charlene Myers joining them and linking her arm familiarly with his. 'Duncan— Renata,' she acknowledged with a cursory smile before her hazel-green eyes came to rest measuringly on the remaining member of their small group. 'Oh, and . . . Mallory. It's darling to have you back with us again, of course, but . . . ' her expression became mock-chiding, 'just because J.B. directed Bren to escort you this evening, doesn't mean you can commandeer all his time, I'm afraid. After all, he *was* supposed to be escorting me!' She glanced up at Bren with an aggrieved pout. 'And already I've been waiting an absolute age for you to arrive! I expect it was Mallory who made you late, but I've something utterly fascinating to tell you and I know I'll just *die* if I don't do so soon!' She began urging him into departing with her.

When Bren didn't immediately fall in with her wishes, however, it was Mallory who spoke up quickly in an attempt to disguise both the undeniable disappointment Charlene's presence had engendered within her, and the annoyance created by the timing thereof that had prevented her from becoming a party to Bren's thoughts for once.

'No, you go with Charlene,' she exhorted with feigned unconcern. Now she knew why he hadn't been prepared to commit himself to her company for the whole evening. 'I'm sure Mr Banfield would hate to have one of his guests expiring in the midst of his party.' A touch of mockery crept into her voice, 'And I've no doubt I'll be able to find *someone* willing to keep me company.' Her chin lifted challengingly.

'Hordes of them, more like!' put in Duncan with a laugh. 'I've never known Mallory short of admirers.'

'And that includes my husband,' chuckled Renata, secure in the knowledge that his appreciation was solely that of a photographer for an outstanding subject, not of an amorous vein.

Although the remarks had Bren's face strangely tightening to a degree, he merely bent his head in acceptance. 'In that case . . . ' He took his departure with Charlene still clinging to his arm as if scared he might suddenly disappear if she let go.

Mallory watched them pensively for a moment and then, under cover of Renata engaging in conversation with a passing couple, she turned back to the man beside her. 'Duncan . . . ' she began with a studiously casual air, 'have you ever heard of a town called Marramaronga Flat?'

'Uh-huh!' He paused slightly, eyeing her enigmatically, before supplying on a rueful note,

'Not that it could strictly be classified as a town, as I understand it. From what I've heard there's little there besides a pub, a general store, a few houses, and a livestock-trucking depot.'

She nodded. 'And would you know just whereabouts it is?'

'Not precisely.' He shook his head, smiling. 'It's somewhere out the back of Bourke, or Wilcannia, or one of those far western towns in New South Wales. I think.' Now his glance became wryly speculative. 'And just why would you be interested in the place where, as it just so happens, Bren Dalton was born, hmm?'

So he knew that! Mallory couldn't control the flush that swept into her cheeks, even as she did her best to fake amazement. 'Goodness, was he? What a coincidence! 'I j-just came across the name yesterday, and—and wondered where it was, that's all,' she stammered. How could she explain that for some unknown reason everything about Bren Dalton had interested her from the time she first met him?

'And in a context totally unrelated to Bren, of course.' His scepticism was almost tangible.

Mallory looked away, biting at her lip. 'All right, so he interests me,' she admitted on a defeated sigh. Her gaze unconsciously strayed across the room to where Bren and Charlene were now standing, and her mouth shaped self-mockingly. 'Not that the reverse applies, of course, as you can see.' Nor was ever likely to, most probably, in view of the annoyance she had caused him, she speculated gloomily.

'For your sake, perhaps it's as well it doesn't.'

Surprise had her eyes widening, and seeing it Duncan half laughed and raised a demurring hand.

'Oh, don't get me wrong. Bren probably has more character than any other man I've ever met. It's just that his outlook regarding women isn't—umm——precisely flattering. In fact, to be quite honest, it's usually downright disdainful.'

'Mmm, so I've noticed,' acceded Mallory, grimacing. 'Although that doesn't appear to have prevented him from—er—succumbing to Charlene's charms, I see.'

'Well, I don't know I'd say he had succumbed, precisely. He may not deprive himself of the most obvious gratification women can supply, and especially not when owing to his own undeniable attraction for the opposite sex—despite his attitude, or maybe because of it—there seem to be any number of them only too willing to provide such satisfaction. Nevertheless, I think it's just as evident none of them have ever succeeded in arousing any deeper emotions within him. Over the years there have been a couple who believed they had been successful in snaring him, only to discover to their dismay just how wrong they were . . . and as I've no doubt will Charlene, too, eventually.' Pausing, he exhaled heavily. 'And that's something I shouldn't like to see happen to you. I've never thought of you as being one for casual affairs.' There was a slight hesitation. 'Unless you've changed your thinking in that regard these days.'

Mallory shook her head. No, she hadn't changed. Her one and only experience within the realms of lovemaking has seen to that. God, what a disappointment it had been! she recalled wryly. She doubted it had been satisfying for either of them, and definitely she hadn't felt any sense of fulfilment or even pleasure. She had simply felt depressed; regretful.

Perhaps she had been too inexperienced, too expectant, she had sometimes thought. But whatever the reason, the fact was that she had never since found herself sufficiently aroused by any man to want to try again.

Now, however, with her thoughts returning to the present, she angled he head enquiringly. 'But do you know why he's so—cynical?'

Duncan shrugged indeterminately. 'Not really. Bren isn't one for giving away information about himself, particularly of a personal nature. Although I strongly suspect that woman in silver and black over there could have a considerable bearing on the matter.'

Swinging around rapidly, Mallory's eyes sought out the woman in question curiously. She found her seated with others grouped about one of the low tables; slim of figure and beautifully turned out, her jewellery obviously expensive but tasteful, her heart-shaped face attractive, and her mid-length brown hair softly curling. But in spite of all the assistance provided by what money could buy, there was still no disguising the fact that she was in her early fifties, and a perplexed frown creased Mallory's forehead. What in heaven's name could her connection be with Bren? And have made him so sceptical, moreover! An unbelievable thought suddenly intruded. Surely, she couldn't have had an affair with him some time, and somehow disillusioned him as a result . . . could she?

'Wh-who is she?' she managed to gulp faintly.

'Her name is Colette Jarvis, and . . . she's his mother.'

Momentarily, Mallory could only stare at him

speechlessly. 'His *mother*!' she gasped finally on recovering her wits. 'But— I assumed . . . ' She shook her head. 'But he never even mentioned anything about her being here! In fact, he hasn't even spoken to her as yet, has he?'

'Not apart from the barest of acknowledgements,' Duncan conceded.

'But—why? And what did you mean about her having something to do with Bren's attitude? Do their personalities clash, or some such?'

'Well, they certainly do that.' His concurrence was drily voiced. 'However, I don't know that's the main casue of their—er—alienation, just the same, because when Bren started attending these social functions, he didn't even know who she was!'

Mallory's gaze was totally uncomprehending. 'Would you mind explaining that?'

'I'm doing the best I can with the little information I have,' he returned on an eloquent note. 'But to put it as briefly as possible, the facts I do know are these. Colette arrived in Melbourne from Sydney some years ago after marrying Lowell Jarvis, the head of Jarvis & Partners of stock-broking renown. Before that, I understand she had been only recently widowed when her considerably older husband—one of Sydney's most influential captains of industry—suffered a heart attack, leaving her as his sole beneficiary. Then, a couple of years ago Bren arrives on the scene—via Banfield's, as you know—and everthing still proceeds quite normally . . . until about six months after Lowell Jarvis had also gone to meet his Maker, whereupon Colette suddenly divulges to Bren that she just happens to be his long-lost mother!' He paused, his mouth crooking expressively. 'I don't know what reception she expected such a disclosure to receive, but I can tell you, I've never seen Bren in such a—well, ominous—mood as he was that night, and he's been completely and utterly unapproachable on the subject ever since.'

Mallory was having trouble taking it all in, and there were so many questions on the tip of her tongue that she hardly knew what to ask first. 'But Bren was born in the outback, not Sydney! Why would she be having a baby out there when she was married to someone in the city? Or did that come first? That she was actually married to, or living with, Bren's father *before* she went to Sydney?' She gave a confused shake of her head. 'It doesn't make sense! I mean, even if that was the case, and she presumably deserted him and his father, since you say Bren didn't even know her when they met later, then why after apparently having ignored him for so many years would she then turn round and reveal their relationship? What's more, how can he be certain she's telling the truth, anyway?'

'As to that, I guess the fact that Bren obviously believes her suggests she must have some proof of her claim,' Duncan reasoned. 'While as for why she suddenly decided to make the disclosure after so long . . . well, I can only speculate as to the reason for that.'

'So . . . speculate,' she invited.

He hunched a deprecatory shoulder. 'Colette not only enjoys the social round but she's also a lavish spender. Unfortunately for her, however, she wasn't the only beneficiary when Lowell died. He had three children from a prior marriage who inherited the majority of his assets.'

'And?'

'I suspect there were two reasons governing the timing of her revelation to Bren. One, because prior to Lowell's death she had no intention of disclosing any such thing; and two, because it wasn't until some months after his death—and with no other likely matrimonial prospect on the horizon—that she suddenly began to worry that her finances might not be quite as inexhaustible as she previously believed.' There was a significant pause. 'And a son who is obviously heading for the top could make a nice, convenient meal-ticket as one gets older, don't you think?'

Mallory gasped, her expression one of appalled disbelief. 'Oh, that's gross! Do you honestly think that's the reason?'

Duncan gave another shrug. 'As I said, I can only speculate, but . . . one thing I have learnt over the years, is that everything Colette does is designed specifically to benefit Colette.'

Mallory's lips compressed and she sighed, but before she could speak Eric joined them, exuding great enthusiasm as a result of her unanticipated presence. Then, with Renata's return also, there was no opportunity to continue the conversation, much to Mallory's disappointment, and shortly they began circulating.

CHAPTER SIX

FOR the next half-hour or so, and with Eric ensuring he remained close beside her as they moved from one group to another, Mallory mechanically went through the ritual of saying all the right things, laughing on cue, making quips, and fending off unwanted male approaches. Not that anyone could possibly have guessed from her manner that she wasn't as content with her surroundings as she appeared to be. And as Bren evidently believed when he unexpectedly appeared next to her.

'Sorry to interfere with your fun,' he began in caustic undertones, and without the slightest sign of remorse in either his voice or the satiric half-smile that encompassed both her and Eric, 'but work is still expected to take precedence, and there's someone here I think it appropriate for you to meet.'

Despite the mockery, Mallory nodded equably. In actual fact, she was grateful for the interruption. Not only did she consider anything connected with her future likely to be decidedly more interesting than the conversation in which she had been participating, but she had also been finding the sheer intensity of Eric's devotion to her a trifle suffocating.

'You see, I told you it wouldn't take long for you to be feeling in your element once more,' Bren went on in the same sardonic accents as they headed across the room after he had assured—with doubtful consideration—a vexed Eric that he was certain

Mallory would be returning to him post-haste as soon as she was able.

'Except that I was *not* feeling in my element! I was merely going through the motions for the sake of politeness,' she said with a dulcet smile. And casting him an even more pointed glance, 'As indeed I presumed you were, too, in view of your earlier comments.' Pausing, she eyed him tauntingly from beneath half-lowered lashes. 'But then . . . perhaps I was wrong, and you really *were* as diverted and engrossed as you seemed in what Charlene's superficial associates, and dear, malicious Stella Ridgway, in particular, had to impart.' She continued swiftly, before the direful look she received in response had a chance to evolve into even more menacing speech. 'Also . . . in future I'll thank you to allow *me* to decide whose company I'm going to seek, post-haste or otherwise, if you don't mind!'

A disparaging curve shaped his mouth. 'Because someone else has caught your eye . . . already?'

'I guess you could say that,' Mallory was prepared to grant, a gleam of humour making her amethyst eyes shine provokingly.

'Yeah—well—I'm afraid you're just going to have to contain your impatience in that regard, all the same!' Bren bit out tautly, cupping her elbow with a forceful hand to increase their pace. 'And quite possibly for some time as well!'

Mallory merely bent her head, and ruefully wondered what his reaction would be if he discovered that, in spite of everything, she still preferred his company to that of any other man there.

None the less, when Bren's attention was distracted late in their conversation with Banfield's financial manager, Mallory made her excuses to the other man and took the opportunity to slip away. She had already noticed Charlene hovering watchfully, determinedly, in the background, and deducing it would only be a matter of time before she began making proprietorial noises again with regard to Bren, decided on the less embarrassing course of choosing when to leave, instead of waiting until forced to depart on being made to feel *de trop*.

At the same time, and after having been enthusiastically welcomed to another circle of old friends, she still couldn't quite prevent her gaze from straying surreptitiously in Bren's direction. His discovery of her departure generated a rapid survey of the room, and an implacable stiffening of his lips when he located her had her mouth going dry even as she elevated her chin to a flouting level.

This action did nothing to relieve the forbidding set of his features, but had him swivelling on his heel and seeking, to her amazement, not Charlene's company as she had expected—and to the tall brunette's obvious chagrin and vexation—but that of a number of men gathered about the outside bar beyond the sliding glass doors that gave on-to the lantern-lit pool area.

Even more unexpected from Mallory's point of view, however, was the fact that, as the evening progressed, the incident proved to be only the first of a number of similar such interruptions she was to experience from Bren. For a variety of reasons he would periodically reclaim her company, until she began to suspect he was simply attempting to unsettle her—doubtless due to his annoyance at having to escort her in the first place—and thereby ensure the evening was as frustrating for her as it evidently was for him.

The fact that his efforts, far from succeeding—at least in the manner he intended—had in actual fact provided the only really enlivening periods of the night, she carefully kept to herself. Simultaneously, the provoking notion that two could play the same game gave rise to some tempting thoughts. So it was that when the string quartet started playing again after supper, this time she deliberately set out to locate him.

She found him with Charlene—one of the few times that girl had managed to secure his exclusive attention, Mallory reflected wryly—but didn't allow that to deter her. In truth, she was a little shocked by the uncharacteristic, and distinctly uncharitable, thoughts that were aroused by the sight of the other girl draped over Bren as they stood by the open marble fireplace.

'I *am* sorry to disturb you,' she began with emphasis, and with about as much regret evident as when he had intervened to commandeer her presence. 'But I was just talking to J.B. . . .' She allowed her words to trail away significantly.

Charlene's lips thinned in exasperation at the interruption, but Bren's expression was harder to interpret. He merely fixed her with a watchful blue gaze and prompted evenly, 'And . . .?'

Mallory hunched a supposedly diffident shoulder, and then followed it with a deliberately provoking half-smile. 'Apparently he's—umm—concerned—that you haven't yet seen fit to dance with me,' she said, though not altogether truthfully. Actually, their employer had only expressed curiosity at their not having participated in the desultory dancing that had been taking place, but she was sure it would only have needed a carefully chosen word or two from her for it to have become concern. He did seem so amenable to to the idea of there perhaps being a relationship between Bren and herself, when all was said and done.

'And, of course, we couldn't possibly allow that—concern to continue,' Bren himself was essaying in partly mocking, partly biting tones.

'I thought it wisest not to,' she granted, dimpling audaciously.

'I'll bet you did!' Pausing, he drew a deep breath. 'Nevertheless, if that's the way it's to be . . .' He shrugged and turned to Charlene, but as if sensing what was coming, that girl was the one to give voice first.

'Oh, this whole thing has gone just too far!' she said irately. 'It was bad enough your being forced to escort Mallory in the first place—not to mention spending so much time with her—but now to expect you to dance with her, too!' Her lips pursed. 'Well, it's just not on! Why should you have to anyway? I mean, what about *my* feelings? Don't they count for anything?' She waited, but when nothing was forthcoming, she flushed and continued stiffly. 'Well, they do to me, I can assure you! So I trust I make myself clear when I say that, if you go ahead and indulge this latest ridiculous whim of Joshua Banfield's, then I won't be waiting patiently for your return, Bren!' Her eyes locked challengingly with his.

It was nothing less than an ultimatum, and Mallory held her breath in trepidation. In view of the aggressive maleness, the unyielding independence, that were so much a part of him, she strongly suspected Bren Dalton wasn't a man to be stood over or intimidated by anyone, let alone a woman, and she was regretfully aware that she was the reason the other girl had been tempted to prove otherwise. Not that it produced the explosion she had anticipated, all the same, for Bren simply flexed a powerful shoulder in a gesture of indifference.

'Suit yourself,' he said as he caught hold of Mallory's arm and began ushering her towards the patio where a few people were dancing.

Charlene promptly crimsoned, and for a time it looked as if she was the one who was going to erupt furiously, but then, with a last glare of glittering intensity, she turned on her heel and stormed in the opposite direction.

'Bren! That was cruel!' Mallory reproved.

He executed another shrug. 'So what makes you think I'm ever kind?'

She frowned. 'Because I believe you can be . . . if you want to be,' she replied on a slightly husky note. 'And she was only . . .'

'Only what . . .?' he cut in harshly. 'Trying to dictate what I do, and with whom?'

Momentarily, she didn't answer as, on reaching the patio, he drew her into his arms to begin moving smoothly to the music, and she was suddenly conscious of his warm, hard length so close to hers, of the powerfully muscled shoulder beneath her fingers, and the fact that her senses were responding to the pleasant sensation his nearness aroused. She had suspected she would enjoy dancing with him, but she hadn't realised to what extent! Now, moistening her lips with the tip of her tongue, she marshalled her thoughts determinedly.

'Well, since you were involved with her . . .'

'Although not any more, I'm relieved to say,' Bren inserted sardonically. His mouth tilted. 'Not that I can see why it should worry you so much, in any case.'

Mallory bit at her lip. 'Because I was the cause of it happening, of course!' Her troubled gaze took in his unconcerned expression and she shook her head in disbelief. 'You don't even—*care*, do you?'

'Not particularly,' he showed no aversion to conceding, and she winced inwardly at the total lack of feeling in his answer. Hadn't his emotions been involved at all? 'She was starting to become too possessive and domineering, anyway, and I didn't need that!'

'Oh, no, naturally not!' she gibed, her own dismayed feelings abruptly taking control. 'After all, you make it abundantly clear you don't *need* anyone or anything . . . full stop!'

To her surprise, and disconcertment, the accusation appeared to provide him with some amusement. 'And if I don't, why should you get so uptight about it?' He arched a graphic brow.

Mallory swallowed and looked away, reluctant to analyse her reasons even for her own enlightenment. 'Because it—it's a selfish way to live,' she faltered unsteadily under his humorous gaze. 'And—and you only ever laugh at me, never with me!' The addition was intended as a distracting recrimination, but the throatiness of her voice made it more of a lament.

Bren bent his head lower. 'Perhaps because I'm not accustomed to finding anything about women particularly amusing.' His lips twisted. 'Certainly Charlene never provided any humorous moments . . . in any form!' He touched a finger to her jaw evocatively. 'So you're already doing better than most, wouldn't you say?' he murmured with a crooked and somewhat self-mocking smile, and Mallory's throat constricted as his warm breath brushed her cheek.

'It's still not very kind, though,' she reproached shakily. It was also such a shame, and a waste, when she so strongly suspected he had such a lot to give

if only he would allow the gentleness and forbearance
she was certain were there to come out, Mallory
mused wistfully. She drew a bolstering breath. 'And
you can't go through the whole of your life distrusting
every woman you meet! You're going to have to
became more than minimally involved, emotionally,
some time!'

'Oh?' He quirked an explicit brow. 'With whom?
You . . . for instance?'

The stark, sardonically uttered words threw Mallory
off balance, as she didn't doubt had been his intention,
and before she could recover she was jolted by the
realisation that he had done no more than define
precisely what she did want.

'And if you didn't glower at me all the time, just
maybe I would endorse that!' she suddenly found
herself declaring in half-flippant, half-challenging
tones.

Bren's grip on her hand tightened, although she was
uncertain whether he was aware of it. 'And what's that
supposed to mean?' he demanded suspiciously. Then,
with his mouth shaping to match the satirically acid
drawl that followed, 'What plan are you hatching now,
that I'm going to regret?'

Even as she wondered if she hadn't had too much
champagne, Mallory slanted him a wry gaze from
between her silky lashes. 'Why do I have to be
hatching anything?'

'Knowing you, it seems more than a possibility!'

'Except that—you *don't* really know me.'

'Although that's all about to change, hmm?' His
eyes took on such a lazily sensuous look that Mallory's
heartbeat accelerated wildly. Lord, what was she
getting herself into? When he looked at her like that he
made her feel weak all over! As Charlene had also felt,

and any number of others before her? came the involuntary—but thankfully rallying—thought.

'I—well—you don't always have to assume the worst, at least, do you?' she evaded unsteadily.

Bren gave the barest of shrugs. 'I guess that all depends,' he drawled.

He didn't say on what it depended, and Mallory deemed it prudent not to enquire. As it was, she was already uncomfortably aware that she was fast losing all semblance of control over her emotions where Bren Dalton was concerned.

'Perhaps you'd care for a cup of coffee, or—or a drink, before you go?' Mallory felt obliged to offer, albeit rather nervously, on Bren having seen her to her hotel-room door after leaving the party a short time later. She was uncertain what his expectations might be as a result of her earlier reckless comments, and even less sure about her own feelings on the matter.

In response, Bren dipped his head briefly. 'A cup of coffee would be most welcome,' he acknowledged on an even note. 'And we have things to discuss, anyway.'

Having opened the door and preceded him into the room, Mallory glanced up at him doubtfully as he closed the door behind them. 'W-we do?' she faltered.

'Uh-huh!'

When nothing more enlightening followed the laconic confirmation, she took the opportunity to put a little more distance between them by making for the built-in counter where the facilities for making tea and coffee were provided.

'Such as?' she asked at length over her shoulder, and as impassively as possible.

'Later,' Bren proposed softly, a hand coming to rest lightly on the nape of her slender neck, making her inhale shakily on realising he had followed her.

Also, she discovered that he had disposed of his jacket and tie, and unfastened the top buttons of his shirt. His casual state of dress gave him a relaxed, slightly rakish air that seemed to fill the room with a virile masculinity, and had her stomach tightening compulsively in response to his indisputable attraction.

'There's something else that needs to be settled first,' he went on in a resonant voice, the hand on her neck inexorably turning her to face him.

'Bren . . .!' Mallory attempted to demur, putting her hands against his chest in defence as he drew her closer. To her despair, though, the feel of the solid, muscled flesh beneath her fingertips only seemed to stimulate a wish for a closer contact, not prevent it, and a stirring heat abruptly coursed through her when she remembered the feel of his tantalising mouth against her own.

'You were the one to suggest I should get to know you better,' Bren murmured before his lips closed over hers.

Well, that wasn't quite what she had said. At least, she didn't think it was. Although right at the moment Mallory wasn't sure she cared. The enticing domination of his sensuous mouth was erasing everything from her mind except the desire to respond. He was arousing feelings she had long since given up expecting ever to experience and, abandoning all thought of protest, she surrendered to them helplessly.

Before she knew it, she was pressing closer to him, her hands tugging his shirt free so that they could explore the firm, smooth flesh beneath. At her touch Bren uttered a raw sound, his muscles hardening convulsively, and then his fingers were digging into her shoulders as he suddenly held her a space away from him. For a moment their glances locked—languid violet with turbulent blue—and Mallory thought she could detect a trace of shock in the depths of the eyes searching hers so intently.

'Wasn't I supposed to want to know you better, too?' she whispered, her gaze turned doubtful.

Bren's grip on her shoulders tightened even further. 'You weren't supposed to make *me* want you to!' he surprised her by abruptly owning in half-groaning, half-growling accents, and pulled her back into his arms as if he couldn't help himself. The action made her aware of just how aroused he was.

Elated at the knowledge, Mallory coiled her arms tightly about his neck, her lips responding willingly to the urgent, consuming demands of his mouth when it claimed hers again. She felt his hands glide down her spine to her hips, moulding her to him more closely, and then return to caress the satiny skin of her back and shoulders in slow, sensual movements.

Mallory's breathing was ragged, and never more so than when he slid the straps of her gown down her arms and, edging down the soft material, bared her creamy breasts to his darkened gaze. High and firm, and surprisingly full for someone of her slender proportions, they swelled invitingly at his touch, the nipples already throbbing erect, and a quivering desire overwhelmed her when he cupped them in his capable hands and then bent to torment them with his lips and tongue.

With a strangled sound, Bren lifted his head, and sweeping her high in his arms carried her blindly to the bed, where he threw back the covers in a careless motion before setting her down gently. Lowering his

head, even as his deft fingers disposed of her garments,
his lips sought the corner of her mouth, her cheek, the
wildly palpitating hollow of her throat, and Mallory
could only lie there, too boneless to move as she
abandoned herself to the tumultuous sensations he was
arousing. She felt breathless with wanting; with
wanting him to satisfy the fiery longings within her that
only he had ever succeeded in inspiring!

Then, suddenly, Bren was settling his muscled
length beside her, his own clothes also discarded now,
and she marvelled at the perfection of his male form; at
his wonderfully smooth skin, so firm and bronzed; at
his powerful chest and shoulders, his long muscular
legs; and the sheer animal vitality that seemed to
emanate from him.

Drawing her closer, he threaded his fingers through
her hair, dislodging her combs, so that the long silken
strands cascaded about her like a silvery waterfall. 'Do
you have any idea just how truly beautiful you are?' he
asked in a husky, wondering voice.

Mallory raised a diffident shoulder and reached up a
hand to caress the chiselled line of his jaw, the contours
of his shapely mouth. 'No more than you are to me,'
she breathed throatily, and with an incredulous shake
of his head he reclaimed her lips with a compulsive
hunger that sent an aching warmth rippling through
her.

Feverishly, Mallory moved against him, her fingers
wandering at will over his hard body, and delighting
not only in simply being able to touch him in such a
fashion, but also the sounds of pleasure her actions
drew from him.

She wanted to arouse in him the same pleasurable
feelings he was arousing so skilfully in her.

Reciprocating, Bren's hands explored her slowly,

seeking and enflaming her most sensitive and responsive areas until the exquisite torment had a hoarse sob breaking from her.

'Bren . . . *please*!' she implored, lifting desire-filled eyes to him. Her body was demanding his possession, demanding it immediately!

Cradling her head between his hands, he kissed her sensuously. 'I know, beautiful . . . I want you, too,' he murmured against her lips in tones made heavy with passion. 'But it will be all the better for waiting.'

Mallory moved her head helplessly. Better? How could it be when her every sense was clamouring for satisfaction? But when he began to use his lips and tongue to retrace the path so recently travelled by his hands, she discovered that the need she had been experiencing paled beside the explosive craving that seared through her now.

As if having deliberately left them until last, Bren turned his attention to her breasts. Cupping their rounded softness in his hands, his fingers teased their pouting nipples until they hardened to swollen peaks, and then he bent to encircle one fervently with his warm mouth.

Unbelievable sensations whipped through Mallory like currents of electricity and she quivered, her body growing wanton as it revelled in his expertise, arching towards him convulsively, her fingers tangling in his dark hair and unconsciously urging him to continue.

His passion mounting, Bren's movements quickened until she was conscious of nothing but him and the mind-shattering desire that boiled in her like molten fire, and carried her with him to a final explosive climax that had her spiralling to the heights of ecstasy.

Shuddering at the breathtaking release of feeling,

Bren caught her to him tightly, burying his face in her neck, and Mallory fastened her arms about his broad shoulders, filled with a wonderment she found difficult to believe. Her only other attempt at lovemaking had left her unprepared for what she had just experienced!

For a time silence reigned in the room, neither of them seemingly able or willing to disturb the satisfaction of the moments they had just shared. Then, as the tempo of his breathing evened, Bren slowly pushed himself up on one elbow to gaze down at her with a hint of confusion in his eyes.

'You haven't done this very often,' he stated heavily rather than questioned, and Mallory's eyes flickered in surprise.

'You could tell?' she asked faintly with a sudden self-consciousness.

His lips twisted wryly. 'I could tell,' he confirmed on an audibly exhaled breath, and suddenly rolled away from her, on to his back, his hands locked behind his head. There was a long pause. 'So why did you do it, Mallory?'

Assailed by a desolating sense of loss at his shifting, she stared at him, perplexed, as she eased herself into a sitting position. Why had she done it? The answer suddenly arrived unbidden. Although no less unexpectedly, nor disturbingly, notwithstanding. Because she was in love with him, of course! But somehow she doubted that would be a reply he would believe . . . or even want to hear, if it came to that, and she bit at her lip in despair. And with that last dispiriting thought came others she miserably supposed she should have considered before surrendering to him so willingly.

Thoughts like . . . hadn't she learnt anything from the happenings of the evening? She had seen how unmoved he had been by the termination of his relationship with Charlene! Had she honestly persuaded herself she might mean anything more to him than that girl had? Oh, sure, she had managed to arouse him, but what did that prove? Merely that he possessed a normal, male sex-drive . . . which she had considerately satisfied in Charlene's stead!

'Well?' Bren's prompting cut into her musings roughly.

Mallory swallowed, but struggling to retain at least some pride, gave a nonchalant shrug—although she had no idea how she managed it. 'Because I felt like it,' she declared with a creditable smile. She dragged in a shaky breath. 'Why did you do it?'

Bren turned his head against one muscular arm. 'I wasn't intending to . . . until your responses made it inevitable.' He showed no compunction in saying this, and she flinched from his words in mortification. 'I'm afraid they made me disregard one of the golden rules. That of never mixing sex with business.' Sitting up in one lithe motion, he swung his feet to the floor and began retrieving his clothes. 'Such involvements always have the possibility of providing . . . leverages.'

Mallory gasped. His implication was all too plain. 'And you think that's why I reacted as I did? In order to influence you with regard to my work?' she choked bitterly.

In the process of dressing, he stopped momentarily and crooked an expressive brow. 'Since you evidently have had only very limited—sexual experience, it raises suspicions.' He resumed shrugging into his shirt, his muscles rippling healthily with every move, and Mallory was disgusted with herself for continuing to admire his magnificent body.

'Only because you're suspicious of everything any

woman does!' she retorted on a flaring note. 'Just because your mother . . .' She gulped in dismay, halting her reckless words, on seeing the bleak and forbidding, closed look that came over his face.

'And just what do you know about my mother?' Bren rasped grimly.

Mallory clutched the sheet to her as if in protection from his stabbing blue gaze. 'I-umm . . .' She shrugged awkwardly. 'You hardly spoke to her all evening.'

If anything, Bren's mouth levelled even further. 'So who told you she was there, in the first place . . . Duncan?'

Was there any point in prevaricating? She nodded. 'He said . . .'

'I don't give a damn what he said!' he interrupted her in stinging tones. 'My mother,' with a pungent inflection, 'is no concern of his . . . or yours! What's more, when and if I feel the need to be psychoanalysed by you, I'll let you know! So until then, I suggest you just keep your ideas on the subject to yourself! Got it?'

Her face leaden, Mallory could only nod strickenly as tears pricked her eyes and desolation billowed through her. Had those electrifying moments they had just shared really meant so little to him?'

'Good!' Bren acknowledged her action tersely. Finished dressing, he moved to collect his jacket, slinging it over his shoulder and heading for the door. 'I'll see you at seven in the morning, then,' he said as he turned back on grasping the handle.

Mallory stated at him in bewilderment. 'Wh-what for?' she just managed to get out past the throat-tightening pain that was gripping her.

'In order to return to Avalon, naturally! Unless, of course, either you're not intending to start work immediately, after all . . . or would rather make the journey back by bus instead of flying.' Strong shades of sarcasm drenched his voice.

And it was that satirical, riling tone that enabled Mallory to find the composure necessary to gibe in return, 'You mean, I'm actually to be forgiven to the extent where I'm not to be forced to endure the tedium of the bus trip home in penance for my sins?'

'Don't get ahead of yourself!' Bren gave a warning, squashing shake of his head. 'Forgiveness doesn't come into it. It's simply a matter of economics. Banfield's are paying you to work . . . not to spend your time journeying all over the State.'

Mallory's brief burst of defiance died as quickly as it had arisen. 'Then of course I'll fly back,' she agreed on a sighing, defeating note.

'And be ready at seven!' he reiterated insistently.

She sucked in a stormy breath. 'I haven't kept you waiting yet!' she defended herself with some asperity.

Bren inclined his head, cynically. 'No . . . but then, there's always a first time, isn't there? And particularly if prompted by thoughts of retaliation.'

'Implying that there's cause for retaliation?'

'I wouldn't advise it!' he said with ominous astringency and, opening the door, took his departure on that warning note.

Now that he was gone, the tears that had been stinging Mallory's eyes, and which she had only just succeeded in holding at bay, spilled on to her lashes. She felt torn and racked with pain by Bren's distrust, and the memory of the unreserved ardour with which she had given herself to him now made her face burn. Curling beneath the sheet in an agony of despair, she pressed her knuckles against her lips as a shuddering sob wrenched free from her throat.

Oh, God! she thought anguishedly. Why had she had to fall in love with him? It hurt too much to be endured.

CHAPTER SEVEN

DURING the weeks that followed, the opportunities
for Mallory to dwell on her emotional state were few
and far between. Initially, because during the day
she was valiantly trying not to be found wanting as a
result of the increased physical exertion demanded
of her, and at night she was just so tired that she fell
asleep immediately her head hit the pillow. These
were circumstances that made her all the more
grateful that, as had been the custom before she
returned, Janet Crowley once again took over the
housekeeping tasks and meal preparation for the
homestead.

From the first day, albeit a little to her surprise,
Bren allowed her a completely free hand. 'You're
being paid to manage the place, not me,' he had
declared, and she had also been relieved to discover
that he didn't intend to be looking over her shoulder,
critically, all the time either. In fact, for the most
part he maintained a rather remote and thoroughly
businesslike manner towards her.

Nevertheless, as the days passed, there were
occasions when he relaxed sufficiently for Mallory to
persuade herself they might almost be approaching a
state of amiable accord—and her spirits would rise
ungovernably each time it happened, even though
her head called her an utter fool. But then, with the
abruptness of someone suddenly flicking a switch, he
would retreat from her once more, leaving her

feeling as if she had been shut out in the cold.

That he also disappeared every weekend, departing Friday evenings and returning Monday mornings, she found impossible to accept equably, too. Not only did it pique her curiosity unbearably as to where he went, but the reason why gave her some frustrating moments as well. She knew he didn't go to Melbourne because they had received a phone call for him one Sunday evening from Joshua Banfield, and she was certain Bren would have advised their head office if he had been in the city.

Her questioning of her stepfather had merely proved he was no wiser on the matter than she was, and so as a last resort she had even attempted to seek the answer from Bren himself, despite strongly suspecting she was wasting her time. She wasn't wrong either, and that in spite of using the pretext of someone or something perhaps requiring his presence urgently with regard to the property.

'I can't see why they would,' he had countered repressively. 'Any decisions concerning Avalon are yours to make. Unless, of course, you're finding the responsibility too much for you.'

Mallory had prudently allowed that to pass without comment, and had altered direction slightly instead. 'But what if it doesn't concern Avalon? What if it's in connection with another Banfield property somewhere?'

'Then since they all have extremely competent managers in charge of them, I'm sure it will be nothing of such magnitude that it can't wait until the following Monday,' Bren had dismissed with finality.

And with that she had had to be content. Or, if not content, then at least suffer it as best she could, while her mind continued to toy with the possible reasons for his weekly absences. These were numerous and varied, but the one that seemed to return more often than the others was the idea that he was visiting someone.

But who? That was what intrigued her most. His father, perhaps? In view of his mother having apparently walked out on them, there would be a close relationship between them as a result, wouldn't there? But if that was the case, he would surely have recognised his mother when they met later—he would have known *something* about her that would have given him a clue!—and yet Duncan had said he had had absolutely no idea who she was.

It was all very confusing and, consequently, usually had her thoughts progressing, if with the greatest reluctance, to her next supposition, that of the person causing his attentiveness being female! It didn't seem to matter that she knew his opinion of her sex made the possibility unlikely, that only recently he had been involved with Charlene. She was only aware of an unsurmountable fear that some girl he had met previously might somehow have succeeded in gaining his trust, and she was wrenched with a grinding despair—and she had to admit it, gnawing jealousy—at the desolating idea.

In an effort to stop such agonising musings, if only temporarily, Mallory threw herself frantically into her work. Christmas came and went in a flurry during the harvest, although still not swiftly enough for Mallory, because the attendant holidays merely gave her the time to lament that Bren had declined the invitation to spend them at Avalon. Yet it did provide the catalyst for her to come to a decision. No matter what the outcome, she was going to find out where he went and why, she determined resolutely. Her emotions just couldn't stand the uncertainty any more, and if it

meant she alienated Bren for ever, well . . . maybe
modelling had its compensations, after all. At least if
she was out of the country she might have a chance to
get him out of her system.

Accordingly, when the last of the wheat had finally
been stripped and delivered to the silos in Nyandra,
she discreetly set about making some enquiries. These
led her to the airstrip, and a good friend from her
schooldays who fortunately saw no reason why she
shouldn't view the copies of Bren's flight plans. Each
time his destination was the same, Mallory discovered:
a property by the name of Kianawah in the far west of
New South Wales. It was not the one where he had
worked before Banfield's had taken it over, she noted,
recalling the different name marked in his personnel
file.

Simply knowing the name of the property, or even
its whereabouts—determined from an atlas when she
returned home—provided little satisfaction as to *why*
Bren kept going there, however, so that in the end she
was forced to conclude that if she was going to find out,
she would have to go there herself.

To this end, Mallory made her plans carefully, first,
by ensuring there was nothing at Avalon that would
require her attention for a couple of days. After all, she
was going to have to drive the three hundred and fifty-
odd miles to reach the property, and in view of the
number of unsealed roads in the area she had noticed
drawn on the map, she very much doubted she would
be able to make the journey there and back in one day.

Then, despite not liking to deceive her stepfather,
but surmising he wouldn't approve of her
intentions—she wasn't even sure she approved of them
herself!—she told Ward she was going to visit a friend
who lived in South Australia, and set off early the

next Monday morning shortly before Bren was due to return. She particularly hadn't wanted to take the chance of running into him at Kianawah! The fact that it was a deliberate invasion of privacy she was contemplating, and something of a kind she had certainly never done before, she tried not to think about. Only . . . how else was she to find out what she so desperately wanted—no, needed, she amended anguishedly—to know?

Heading north across the border, Mallory skirted the edges of the flat and very hot saltbush and grass-covered Old Man Plain, and then crossed the Murrumbidgee River. Above her the sun was a white-hot ball in the endless washed blue of the sky, the air blowing into the vehicle ony adding to the all-pervading, stifling heat that seared the lungs and had her shirt clinging to her back with perspiration. Although the Wimmera enjoyed hot weather, it hadn't normally the ferocious intensity of this, she mused ruefully.

Nor was the countryside at all similar. This was no gently undulating landscape graced with numbers of trees. It was mainly flat, far-reaching plains supporting low-growing shrubs, and where only the occasional mulga-topped ridge interrupted the never-ending view.

It was the middle of the afternoon when Mallory finally reached Dinjerra, the tiny township nearest Kianawah, and after seeking directions from the talkative café proprietor on how to locate the property, she was soon on her way again.

However, on making the last turn after another twenty or so miles, and eventually reaching the gate that bore the station's name emblazoned on it, she brought her stepfather's car to a halt. Instead of making any move to open it, she sat staring at it doubtfully, her lip caught between her teeth, and the full import of her position only then suddenly descending on her.

So just what did she do now that she *had* found where Bren went each weekend? Bowl up to the homestead and demand to be told *why* he did so? Oh, God, how could she have been so stupidly, impulsively unthinking as to believe merely locating the property would provide any answers? She doubtless would have been better advised to continue talking to the café proprietor and attempting to pump him for the information she wanted! With a forlorn sigh, she bowed her head against her hands as they rested on the steering-wheel.

Then, all at once, the sound of another vehicle reached her, and on raising her head, Mallory found a dust-covered yellow ute pulling to a stop alongside her. A lean, grey-haired, and weatherbeaten man in his middle sixties alighted and made his way over to her with a casual gait.

'You need any help? You lost?' he enquired in a gruff voice, frowning, and his shrewd hazel eyes surveyed her intently from beneath the brim of his battered bush hat.

Mallory shook her head agitatedly, and dragged up a weak half-smile. 'No, to both questions . . . thank you. I—I was just . . . having a bit of a rest, that's all,' she offered lamely.

He nodded slowly, but somehow she gained the impression it was more to himself than in acknowledgement of what she had said. 'It looked more than that to me,' he let his thoughts be known, and promptly fixed her with another penetrating gaze.

'In fact, I reckon I wouldn't be far wrong if I said . . . you're Mallory, aren't you?'

So totally unexpected was his deduction that she had no time to prevent the stunned shock she experienced from registering betrayingly on her features, and the old man nodded again, with evident satisfaction this time.

'Yeah, I thought so,' he said laconically.

'B-but how did you know?' she faltered, nonplussed. It seemed futile to deny it.

'The Victorian plates on your car first set me wondering. They're pretty rare round here, and especially this far off the beaten track,' he disclosed in his slow, deliberate manner. 'But mostly, I guess, it was your face.' He uttered a dry chuckle. 'I may only be an uneducated old bushman, but I still know a good looker when I see one, and since I'd been told you had the face of an angel . . . well, it wasn't all that difficult to put two and two together.'

One particular phrase had Mallory's eyes widening. She couldn't imagine why Bren would have discussed her with this man, but . . . 'That's how Bren described me?' she couldn't help but probe with a certain amount of disbelief.

'Uh-huh!' There was a pause and he executed a deprecatory shrug. 'Along with the view that you also possessed the principles of a scheming con-man.'

'Oh!' Mallory's face flamed. 'How dare he?' she fumed, amethyst eyes sparkling. 'They are nothing of the kind, and—and his are always above reproach, I suppose!' Her voice turned sardonic. 'Was it principled of *him* to spread such prejudiced lies about me to all and sundry?'

'Not all and sundry, lass,' the old man corrected heavily. 'Only me.'

Well, at least that was something, she supposed, although it still did little to dispel her resentment until a random thought dismissed it altogether, and she gasped, 'You're not his father, by any chance, are you?'

He shook his head. 'No, his old man's been dead for going on twenty years now. He was crushed to death while working cattle in some yards up in the Territory. He was a drover, you know.'

'No, I didn't know,' Mallory replied wistfully. How could she have done when Bren was so close-mouthed about himself? 'But I'm sure I've already taken up too much of your time, Mr—er . . .' She had no choice but to leave it unsaid. 'And I guess I'd better be making tracks as well before . . .'

'But surely you intend coming up to the homestead,' he interposed with a frown. 'Else why did you drive all the way up here?'

Mallory gave a mirthless half-laugh. 'I was asking myself that question when you arrived!' she quipped on a self-mocking note.

He exhaled deeply. 'In that case, I think you'd better come on up to the homestead.' He paused, 'You'll need somewhere to stay the night, in any event.'

'Oh, but I couldn't possibly . . .' she immediately began to protest, and then stopped on assimilating the full implication of his words. 'You mean . . . you live here? You own Kianawah?'

'Well, I manage it, I guess you could say,' he qualified. 'Although Bren makes all the major decisions, of course.'

'He does?' she said confusedly.

She found herself on the receiving end of a partly unbelieving, partly incredulous gaze delivered from beneath lowered brows. 'Well, you must have known he owned it, otherwise why did you come here?'

Momentarily, Mallory couldn't speak as her spirits lifted magically. It was a property Bren had been visiting every weekend, not a person? And even more comfortingly, not a female person!

'No, I had no idea he owned it,' Mallory replied at length. A wryly regretful curve shaped her lips. 'Bren—has never told me anything about himself. But then, considering the opinion he apparently has of me, I guess it really would be too much to expect him to confide in me, of all people.' She tried to sound flippant by laughing, but her voice quavered treacherously, and she dropped her gaze in embarrassment.

The old man rubbed his chin and grunted. 'Yeah—well—Bren's always been one for keeping things to himself.' He hesitated. 'He had a hard start in life, and that's made him a hard man. At least, on the surface, that is. Beyond that, there's a different person.' He cleared his throat self-consciously, as if regretting having said so much, and began turning away. 'Anyhow, I'll lead the way to the homestead, and you can just follow me, all right?'

This time Mallory didn't protest, but nodded willingly. Whoever the man was, he evidently knew as much about Bren as anyone did, if not more, and it was in the hope of gaining such information that she had driven all this way, after all. The repercussions that might follow from her visit when Bren came to learn of it, as she supposed he would, she studiously refused to contemplate for the present. She would deal with that problem tomorrow, she decided staunchly.

It was some miles further before they reached the homestead, and as she drove Mallory now looked about her with greater interest. At least the countryside was a little more varied now, she noticed, as a few cypress pines, acacias, and coolibahs made their appearance. She also noted that here, too, were the contoured earth banks for water-spreading that were to be employed at Avalon, probably even more necessary in this region of less rainfall, she surmised. As well, there was a considerable amount of new fencing to be seen, and numerous young trees strategically planted, so that long before they arrived at the somewhat dilapidated old veranda-encircled homestead—parts of which were also obviously undergoing reno-vation—she had come to a conclusion.

'I guess Bren has only recently bought the property,' she hazarded as she followed the old man up the rickety steps on to the uneven veranda.

'Mmm, a couple of years, that's all.' He paused for a moment, looking out past the few trees that shaded the house and various outbuildings to the vast sweep of the land beyond, and then released a noisy sigh. 'It was very run down, and it takes a fair bit of money, as well as hard work, to get it producing again. Still, we're getting there. It takes time.' He abruptly slanted her a considering gaze. 'But if Bren didn't tell you about the place, how did you find out about it?'

Mallory bent her head, unable to stop the colour rising in her cheeks. 'I—umm—checked his flight plans in Nyandra,' she divulged truthfully, if in a rather abashed murmur.

'Why?'

She swallowed nervously, feeling like a fly under a microscope beneath his narrowed, assessing glance, but suspected that honesty was still likely to achieve more with this man than evasion. 'Because I was interested—and since he obviously didn't mean to

volunteer the information . . .' She shrugged
deprecatorily.

'Was there any reason he should have done?'

'From his point of view, apparently not!' she
quipped in an effort to disguise the barb of pain that
speared through her at his question.

Briefly, he continued to watch her unwaveringly,
and then he turned for the front door, his lips
compressing into a dour line. 'Well, something's been
eating at him these last weeks! He doesn't often spend
every weekend here—especially when he's so busy for
Banfield's—and not even if his vacation has been
deferred!'

Mallory drew a sharp breath and hurried after him,
squinting to adjust her eyesight from the sunlit glare
outside to the dimly lit hallway as she followed him
down it. 'Just what are you trying to say, Mr—er . . .'

'Oliver—Lew Oliver's the name,' he said. 'But
you'd better just call me Lew. Everyone else does.
While as for the other . . .' He came to a sudden halt,
shaking his head. 'Hell, I'm not sure what I'm trying
to say! I just know that something's giving him a bad
time . . . and you're the only female he's ever
mentioned to me by name! And I know for a fact that
he's been involved with a few before today!' He
resumed stomping down the passageway to an
enormous old country-style kitchen—complete with
combustion stove, tall wooden dressers, and a long
scrubbed table capable of seating eight or more—at the
back of the building.

Mallory trailed after him more slowly, torn with
conflicting emotions. No matter how much she wanted
to believe that it was an attraction for her, however
slight, that was affecting Bren, she just couldn't bring
herself to accept that as the cause. Oh, sure, he had

sometimes made her feel as if he wasn't entirely *un*attracted to her, and she was sure their lovemaking had been as gratifying for him as it had been for her. At the same time, though, she was equally aware that that didn't necessarily mean his emotions had been more than superficially involved. In fact, everything seemed to point to just that being the case. He had mistrusted her on sight, and now being forced to accept her at Avalon was what was really rankling him.

'Have a seat, and I'll make us a pot of tea,' said Lew as she joined him. Lifting the lid of the large, cast-iron pot set on one side of the stove, he gave the contents a stir, and then opened the smaller of the stove's two doors to add some wood to the fire within. 'Or maybe you would rather something cold to drink. There's orange juice and Coke in the fridge.'

'No, tea will be more than welcome, thank you,' Mallory replied as she seated herself at the long table. The size of it prompted her to enquire, 'How many people altogether are there on the property, Lew?'

'Oh, most times there's only Richie and me. He's our young stockman. You'll meet him at dinner,' he declared, putting a heavy, blackened kettle of the same vintage as the iron pot on the hottest part of the top-plate. 'If Bren's not here and we need more help, we hire a feller or two from town to give a hand. Since I'm also the cook, we all eat here together, though.'

Mallory nodded, her thoughts inexorably returning to the subject that had brought her there. 'You've known Bren a long time, haven't you, Lew?' she couldn't refrain from probing.

He stopped his bustling search for mugs and spoons, and nodded. 'Since he was twelve.' His mouth sloped whimsically. 'Although he was claiming to be fifteen at

the time.' That three-year discrepancy in his personnel
file! Mallory thought immediately. 'Still, it was some
months before even I realised he wasn't,' Lew
continued. 'He was a strapping kid for his age, and he
could do a man's work. I might add, he was also a
damned sight more difficult to get any information
from about himself than he is now! Oh, yes, he was a
real hard nut to crack in those days, all right!'

Mallory's eyes clouded sorrowfully. 'But what made
him that way, Lew?'

Before answering, he crossed to the table, resting his
work-roughened hands on the back of the chair
opposite her, and bending slightly as he viewed her
with that appraising gaze of his. 'You're very curious
about him, aren't you?'

Mallory bent her head. 'I said it was because—I
was interested that I came.'

'Mmm, I know what you said, but . . . just how far
does your interest go, Mallory?' There was a pause.
'Do you love him?'

The sheer abruptness, and the unexpectedness, of
the question had her swallowing convulsively. But as
she had also sensed previously that Lew wasn't the
person to try to deceive either, her head lifted to an
almost defiant angle. 'Yes!' she admitted on a fierce
note, and then her eyes began to water uncontrollably
and she covered her face with her hands. 'Oh, God,
yes! Right from the first, he attracted me more than
any man I've ever met, and now I can't imagine life
without him!' She choked back a sob. 'He's also the
only man I've never been able to tell just exactly how
he feels about me in return. One moment I think there
might be some feeling there, and the next I have
absolutely no idea. He's just so hard to reach, and
gives so little away!'

'Yes—well—he's just wary, lass, that's all.' A comforting hand patted her awkwardly on the shoulder, startling her because she hadn't realised Lew had moved. 'You might understand better if I perhaps tell you why.'

Mallory nodded and wiped the tips of her fingers across her damp lashes and cheeks. 'I'm sorry to have become so emotional,' she apologised self-consciously. 'I don't usually let go like that, especially in front of strangers, but . . .' The sound of heavy footsteps approaching down the hallway had her breaking off defensively.

'Lew! What's the meaning of that car out the front?' The somewhat tersely barked enquiry preceded the man's appearance, but the voice had Mallory's eyes rounding in alarm and her face turning ashen.

'Bren?' she managed to get out in a strangled croak, staring at Lew in shattered disbelief.

He frowned at her evident trepidation. 'But I thought that's why you . . .' He expelled a heavy breath. 'He rang Avalon early this morning to say he wouldn't be returning until tomorrow,' he explained quickly.

But she had left even earlier! Mallory closed her eyes briefly in despair, and then Bren's tall form was entering the room—promptly seeming to dominate everyone and everything in it with a raw masculinity and a distinctly aggressive demeanour. Mouth hard, his expression cynical, he took in the scene at a glance.

'Christ! Don't tell me she's working her wiles on you, too, now!' he grated contemptuously, eyeing the older man's hand still resting on Mallory's taut shoulder. 'While as for you . . .!' His glance dropped to the drained face turned to him so apprehensively. 'Directly I saw the vehicle I knew it could only have been Ward or you, so just what are you doing here, Mallory?' He shook his head savagely before she could begin to formulate a reply. 'No, don't bother to tell me! Unless it concerns Avalon, I'm not interested enough to care! I don't know how you found out about Kianawah, or what made you think you might be welcome here, but the door's that way!' He stabbed a finger towards the hall. 'You can leave right *now*!'

As white as it had been previously, Mallory's face now crimsoned with humiliation as she hurriedly stumbled to her feet. 'Y-yes, of—of course. I'm s-sorry,' she quavered, wanting only to escape in order to nurse to herself the grief his vehement dismissal had caused.

'*No!*' It was Lew who uttered the forceful dissent, his hand on her arm that brought her shaky steps to a halt. 'She's my guest, and I say she's welcome to stay!' He glowered at the younger man challengingly.

Momentarily, their gazes clashed, and then with an exasperated shake of his head Bren let loose a muttered string of fluent curses before stalking from the room.

With his departure a little of Mallory's tenseness left also, although not her need to escape, and as a result she turned to the man beside her with a regretful look. 'I'm sorry, Lew, but I think I'd better leave, all the same,' she murmured throatily. 'You've been very kind, and I do appreciate your stopping Bren from—ordering me off the property, but I don't want to create any trouble between the two of you. Besides . . .' she sighed dispiritedly, 'he couldn't have made it more plain what he thinks about my being here.' She began making for the door.

'But that was only because he wasn't expecting to see you here!' Lew put in urgently. 'Give him time to become used to the idea!'

Mallory shook her head and increased her pace. If she didn't get away soon she would end up embarrassing herself, and him, by crying again. 'No, Lew. I—I'm sorry,' she quavered. 'It's not time he wants . . . just me off Kianawah.' With another anguished shake of her head she broke into an unsteady run.

Behind her, Lew gave an exasperated grunt, and then she heard him bellowing, 'Bren! If that girl leaves this property because of you, so help me I'll lay my stockwhip about your back!'

What Bren had to say in reply, if anything, Mallory didn't hear as she hurried down the veranda steps and across to her car. Not that she expected the threat to have any effect. She didn't doubt Bren's desire to see her gone would surmount any wish Lew might have for her to stay. Consequently, it came as something of a shock when, on just having started the engine, she found her door being dragged open and Bren bending to turn the ignition off again.

'Out!' His curtly voiced instruction had all her feelings of despondency, disappointment, and despair giving way to a flaring anger that he should now, conversely, be as good as ordering her to stay, and she glared at him rebelliously.

'No! I didn't come here to be . . .'

'But you are here, and Lew says you're staying!' he cut in tautly.'

'Well, I say I'm not, and . . . Oh!' The partly surprised, partly furious exclamation was forced from her as steely fingers gripped her and, despite her efforts to break free, she was hauled unceremoniously from the vehicle. 'No!' she continued to protest stormily, struggling violently against the hands that still restrained her. 'You can't make me stay if I don't want to!'

Bren's grim features took on a sardonic aspect. 'I thought I just had!'

That his superior strength afforded him the opportunity to mock her as well had Mallory seething and wanting somehow, anyhow, to wipe that infuriating self-assurance from his devastatingly masculine face. Spontaneously, she lashed out with her open hand, only to have it caught in a grip like iron before it could reach its objective.

'I wouldn't recommend it!' Bren counselled in goading accents. 'Striking the boss usually constitutes a sacking offence.'

Indignation had Mallory's breasts rising and falling sharply. 'And what about harassing employees?' she fired back. 'Or doesn't that count?'

'Harassing?' He raised an implicit brow. 'The shoe's on the other foot, isn't it, sweetheart? *You* came here uninvited!'

'Much to my regret, I can assure you!'

'Yeah—well—that's as may be, but in the meantime . . .' He kneed the door of the car shut and began pulling her in the direction of the homestead.

'No!' she shouted once more, resuming her struggles. 'I'm not giving you the excuse to make Lew's life a misery as well, just for saying I was his guest!'

'Me make *his* life a misery!' Bren stopped in order to expostulate in ironic disbelief. 'You heard what he said!'

Mallory pressed her lips together deprecatingly. 'That was merely an idle threat!'

'The only other time he said it, it wasn't!'

Diverted by some nuance in his tone, she gazed up at him curiously. 'You mean, he really has taken a

stockwhip to you before now?' Somehow the idea
appealed to her wounded sense of justice.

'Mmm, I was sixteen at the time, and told him that
if I wanted to go into town with the rest of the men and
get drunk, I would, and if he didn't like it, he could go
to hell.' The cast of his mouth became wryly
pronounced. 'He laid into me.'

Simultaneously, Mallory was struck by two
thoughts. Most important, the realisation that for the
first time he had actually, voluntarily, divulged
something about his past to her! Although it had been
a hard way to achieve it, she had to admit. The
second, she thought might prove even more revealing
regarding the man himself, and she put it into words in
the faint hope of that being so.

'You couldn't have stopped him?' she asked
tentatively. After all, by that age he would surely have
been twice the size of Lew and, she didn't doubt, well
able to defend himself.

Bren flexed a drill-covered shoulder impassively. 'I
could have. I just didn't consider the cost worth it.'

'The cost?'

'Don't be dense, Mallory!' he derided in a
roughening change of tone. 'You don't fight a man
who's been like a father to you, and who you really
respect more than anyone else on this earth! Of course
I could have taken the whip off him, but he wouldn't
have surrendered it willingly, fifty years of age or not,
and that meant he could have been hurt! I wasn't
prepared to take that chance, especially not when I
figured I was probably only getting what I deserved for
having smart-mouthed him in the first place.'

Lucky Lew to have managed to have Bren think
that much of him, mused Mallory enviously. Aloud,
and in return for his derision, she ventured to taunt, 'I

see, so it was fear of having to suffer the same again that made you come after me?'

Briefly, Bren's blue eyes glittered, sending a frisson of apprehension racing down her spine, and then his expression turned coolly mocking. 'You appear to have overlooked the possibility that I simply wouldn't consider you worth it.'

Mallory pressed her lips together to halt their betraying trembling. 'Then I sincerely hope Lew carries out his threat!' she retorted, albeit somewhat huskily, starting to struggle against his hold once more. If she could just get inside her car and lock the door, he wouldn't be able to prevent her from leaving.

'More than likely,' granted Bren in something of a growl. 'But it's not going to be today!' As if finally losing all patience, he suddenly bent and hoisted her over his shoulder like a bag of wheat, and made for the homestead with an easy, loose-limbed stride that gave no indication of the indignantly protesting and squirming form he was carrying.

CHAPTER EIGHT

INSIDE the kitchen once more, Mallory was deposited none too gently on to the chair she had occupied only a short time before.

'Next time you'd better do your own collecting,' Bren advocated drily to Lew.

'I doubt I could employ such—finesse—to persuade her to return,' retorted the older man on a meaningfully ironic note.

A mocking grin briefly etched its way across Bren's strong features, and Mallory's heart leapt waywardly in response. Damn him for being able to affect her emotions so effortlessly! she railed helplessly, and turned her back to him, the better to display the resentment his arbitrary treatment had aroused.

'Yeah—well—she's all yours now,' Bren drawled. 'Just keep her out of my way, that's all.' His voice roughened fractionally.

Unable to resist the challenge of the tacit censure, Mallory swivelled to face him again rapidly. 'I was never intending to get in your way!' she flared acrimoniously.

'Well, that's comforting to hear, at least!' the sarcastic gibe came swiftly. 'God only knows to what extent you might have disrupted the smooth running of my life if you had intended to do so!' Spinning on his heel, he paced tensely from the room.

Mallory turned back with a sigh, half smiling at Lew in acknowledgement of the mug of steaming tea he placed before her. 'I think it would have been better if you had just let me leave,' she said heavily as she added milk and sugar to the dark liquid and slowly stirred it.

He cast her a penetrating glance from beneath his bristling brows as he once more attended to the pot on the stove. 'And I thought you said you wanted to know more about him! Or was that just all talk?'

'No!' she denied indignantly. 'It's just that I get the feeling it's all rather . . .' she hunched a despondent shoulder, 'in vain.'

'OK, if that's your decision.' Lew shrugged and returned his attention to the pot.

'I didn't say that! I only meant . . .' She broke off, wondering why, in view of Bren's attitude, it was still important to her, and yet knowing incontrovertibly that it was. 'Lew, tell me what you know about his mother,' she said quietly.

For a time she didn't think he meant to reply, but then, to her relief, he exhaled heavily and said, 'From that, I presume you've met her?'

Mallory shook her head. 'No, someone pointed her out to me during a party at Joshua Banfield's house, that's all.' She hesitated. 'Bren barely acknowledged her.'

Lew gave a contemptuous snort. 'That's hardly surprising! If I were him I wouldn't even be that civil!' Leaving the stove, he took a seat opposite her at the table and poured himself some tea before continuing. 'You see, his mother—no, change that to the woman who gave birth to him, since that's about all she did for him!—would have to be one of the most selfish and calculating women it's been anyone's misfortune to meet! I mean, not only did she desert her husband and only child—the latter only two at the time—in favour of a wealthy tycoon who happened to be passing through town, but she couldn't even wait until her husband returned from his droving-trip in order to tell him. No, she just dumped her child on the family next door—who were under the impression they were merely baby-sitting for the afternoon—and left that very day without so much as leaving a note!' His lips curled with disgust. 'Apparently she considered her looks deserved better than an out-of-the-way place like Marramaronga Flat, and since she had always hankered after the city lights, she didn't intend to allow anything or anyone to deprive her of the opportunity to realise her aspirations!'

'And the man she left with was willing to let her just leave her child like that?' Mallory gasped incredulously.

Lew uttered a mirthless half-laugh. 'You forget, I said she was calculating. And definitely too scheming to let slip knowledge of that importance, I'll be bound. I doubt he even knew she had a child.'

Mallory shook her head, frowning. She knew it did happen, of course, but she still found it difficult to believe any woman could be so unfeeling towards her own offspring. Although more important at the moment . . . 'And Bren? What happened to him after that?'

Lew shrugged. 'Well, naturally he was too young for his father to take with him on his droving-trips, so he was left in a children's home, in the nearest town that had one. From there he was farmed out to various foster families over the years, where his old man would visit him when he could.'

'That couldn't have been much of a life,' Mallory reflected with a sigh.

'Particularly not when I gather women, of one age

or another, once again made a couple of his experiences not over happy ones either.'

Sipping at her tea, she nodded thoughtfully. 'But you said you've known him since he was twelve?'

'Mmm, that was when his old man was killed. By that time, though, he'd had enough of being shifted from here to there and back again, so rather than wait around to find out what the authorities had in mind for him, he took off back into the bush and got himself a job on the station where I was head stockman.' Lew took a mouthful of his tea, his expression turning reminiscent. 'It was months before I could get him to admit he wasn't the fifteen years he was claiming to be, and it was even longer before I could persuade him to finish his schooling by correspondence at least. Bully him into doing it, was more like!' he added with a wry half-laugh. 'But it was worth it. It paid off for him in the end.'

Mallory surveyed his lined face meditatively. 'You think a lot of him, don't you, Lew?' she said softly at length.

His brows lifted. 'Why wouldn't I? He's given me a home here when I was too old to be kept on by anyone else.'

But it went deeper than that, Mallory realised. It wasn't only gratitude she could see on his face. There was pleasure and pride, and loyalty, too. For if, as Bren had said, Lew had been like a father to him, then it was also more than evident that Bren was like a son to Lew as well. As a result, her curiosity had her asking, 'You never had a family of your own?'

Lew shook his head. 'No, I never got round to getting married, and any other relatives I may have once had are now either dead, or I've lost touch with them over the years and don't know where they are,' he replied matter-of-factly.

Mallory nodded and gave him a half-smile. 'Well, thank you for telling me about Bren, anyway. It explains a lot. And since you'd never even met me before today . . .' She released an expressive breath.

'Yes, well, as long as you don't give me cause to regret having told you!' His tone shortened suddenly. 'You were the one to come here today, and I believed you when you said you loved him. But if you do the wrong thing by him, then I'm telling you straight, you'll wish you hadn't ever come here, because it will be *me* you'll be answering to! And I don't do things by halves!' he warned darkly.

Mallory gulped, never doubting for a minute that he wouldn't be as good as his word, but before she could attempt to reassure him, he was continuing, although in more moderate accents, she was glad to note.

'So long as you remember that.' He rose to his feet in order to stir the pot on the stove once more. 'I hope you've no objections to stew for dinner. It's probably not what you're used to, but it's filling, and when we're out all day it's easiest just to put it on in the morning and let it simmer.'

Grateful to be back on a less contentious topic, Mallory sniffed appreciatively the appetising aroma that was permeating the room. 'It if tastes as good as it smells I'm sure I won't have any complaints.' She tilted her head to one side. 'But what makes you think it's not what I'm used to?'

'Bren said you were an international model.'

'*Was!*' she interjected to stress with a grimace. Didn't he ever intend to accept that she really had finished with that part of her life?

'Well . . .' Lew shrugged deprecatorily. 'After those fancy restaurants and hotels and all you no doubt visited, I just figured you'd probably eat fancier, too.'

'Although not since I've been home at Avalon, of course,' she replied drily. 'As I'm sure you're aware through having worked for the company yourself, Banfield's are not so generous as to provide the wherewithal necessary to keep their employees dining on caviar, truffles, and pheasant under glass.'

'No, they certainly don't do that!' he agreed with a chuckle, and the conversation moved on to general topics.

Shortly afterwards, Richie Mayo, their stockman, put in an appearance. An easy-going young man of some twenty years of age, he made his appreciation of Mallory plain, and kept her entertained until it was time to prepare for dinner.

Of Bren, there had been no further sign, and as she donned a simple, square-necked cotton dress after showering, Mallory felt her stomach constricting at the thought of their impending meeting. Did he mean to make his displeasure at her presence known as harshly as before, and to Richie now as well, or did he intend to ignore her altogether? Either way it presaged an uncomfortable evening at best, a downright embarrassing one at worst, and her apprehension mounted accordingly as she finished dressing and nervously made her way back to the kitchen.

However, as it turned out, and much to her relief, Bren followed neither course. Whether out of deference to Lew or not, Mallory couldn't be certain, but he chose to be more of a cynical observer, occasionally making some mocking rejoinder, but for the most part contemplating the company with a slightly sardonic regard.

Richie, on the other hand, was only too pleased to claim Mallory's attention. In his engaging manner

he plied her with questions, told humorous anecdotes,
happily volunteered information about his work on the
station, and with Lew's help, generally made the
conversation both interesting and amusing. At first,
Mallory responded with constraint, all too conscious of
Bren's vital and scrutinising presence at the head of the
table. But as the evening wore on, she gradually began
to relax and answer the other two in bantering kind.

At least, that was until something Richie said had
her breaking into spontaneous laughter for the second
time in as many minutes, and her sparkling eyes
chancing to collide with the flaring blue of Bren's gaze
jolted her with dismaying realisation. He was seething!
Gone altogether now was the indolent pose, replaced
by an explosive tenseness that appeared to be growing
by the second, and which promised such a devastating
eruption that she shivered compulsively.

As for the reason governing his so forebodingly
altered mien, she could only suppose it riled him that
she was finding something pleasant about her visit to
Kianawah, or that the other two men were vexingly
making it so. She didn't doubt that it was she who
would suffer the consequences, nevertheless. And
before too much longer! she surmised shakily, judging
by the uncompromising slant to his firmly moulded
mouth, and the tension he continued to exude which
seemed to vibrate in the air between them.

As a result, she wasn't altogether surprised, when it
came time to say goodnight and she began making her
way to her room, that Bren caught her up before she
could reach her door. It did nothing to lessen her
nervousness, or resentment, when he arbitrarily
hustled her inside and, raking her with a disquieting
gaze, leant back against the panelled door with his

arms folded across his broad chest.

'Just what do you think you're doing?' she demanded rapidly in tones of affront.

'What am *I* doing?' he countered disbelievingly in a low voice. Dangerously low. 'The question is . . . just why the hell are *you* here, Mallory? I presume it wasn't solely with the intention of setting out to captivate Lew and young Richie!' His voice became larded with scorn.

Deliberately avoiding his first question, she protested the last in lieu. 'That's not fair! I didn't set out to—to captivate them at all!'

'Then why are you here?' He started towards her with a determined tread.

Mallory moistened her lips and took a couple of steps backwards. 'I thought you said you didn't care!' She pounced on the evasion agitatedly.

Bren brushed it aside with a shake of his head. 'So what was it you were after, Mallory?' he persisted roughly, and seeming to tower over her. 'More of . . . this?' He caressed the soft underside of one of her breasts in a contemptuously insolent gesture.

Shock held Mallory immobile, her breath coming in ragged gasps. Shock at his action, and shock at the undeniable response of her body as the soft flesh immediately swelled against his hand. The atmosphere was suddenly electric, and from the look on Bren's face she was aware that the moment had affected him unexpectedly as well. For a fraction of a minute their startled gazes locked, and then Mallory shook her head helplessly.

'Bren . . . please!' she entreated in an anguished whisper. 'Don't be cruel!'

'Cruel? Unfair?' he repeated hoarsely, his hands sinking into the silvery strands of her hair on either

side of her head. 'Were you kind or fair coming here
uninvited, prying into my life, recalling memories I
could have done without, stirring a man's senses . . .?
God, how you stir the senses!' With a defeated groan,
he set his mouth to hers in a long, ravaging kiss that
made Mallory's senses swim. 'You invade a man's
mind so that his every thought, his every feeling, is
bound inextricably to you!' he continued thickly
against her parted lips. 'I swore to myself that I
wouldn't be taken in by a breathtaking face and an
alluring smile, but you still make me ache with the
memory of the pleasure only your warm and willing
body has ever managed to give mine, and just the
thought of making love to you again has been driving
me nearly mad!'

Mallory trembled. Did he realise what he was
saying—what could he mean? Or was it merely her
wishful thinking reading into his words what she so
desperately wanted to believe? His only mention had
been of desire, not love, but then maybe that wasn't so
surprising considering the years of distrust that needed
to be overcome. Perhaps time would provide the key,
while in the meantime . . . She only knew she couldn't
deny her love for him, even if she wasn't yet confident
enough to reveal it. Her heart yearned for him, and
she wanted him as much as he apparently wanted her.
At that moment, nothing else seemed to matter, and
sliding her arms around him, she pressed invitingly
closer to the taut outlines of his muscular form.

'Bren, I came here because I couldn't get you out of
my mind either, and—and . . . oh, God, I want you
again, too!' she confessed.

Releasing a shuddering breath, Bren crushed her to
him tightly, his lips claiming hers with a searing
hunger that ignited fires in her veins, and a consuming

passion that engulfed them both. Mallory lost track of time and place as she gave herself up to the seductive tongue probing her mouth, the skilful hands that caressed every inch of her.

Gasping, Mallory clutched at his dark head, urging his mouth back to hers, wanting him to kiss her. She sighed with pleasure when he at last moved over her, and wave after wave of ecstatic feeling washed over her in a rapturous union that left them both spent and shaken.

Their passion quenched, Bren continued to hold Mallory close in his arms, her head pillowed on his warm shoulder, their legs still entwined, and she sighed contentedly. She didn't want to consider the implications of her actions—or his—just yet, but the momentary spurt of anxiety one particular memory evoked must somehow have communicated itself to Bren for he turned his head to hers watchfully.

'What's wrong, beautiful?' he asked in a soft but slightly guarded murmur.

Unsettled a little by his alertness, and tensing apprehensively, Mallory averted her gaze. 'Last time, you accused me of—of going to bed with you only in order to influence you with regard to my work,' she said throatily. Now her amethyst gaze returned to his anxiously. 'It wasn't true then, and it's not true now! But I couldn't help wondering if you meant to . . .' she swallowed, 'make the same charge again.'

Bren's arms tightened about her imperceptibly as he shook his head. 'No, not again,' he denied heavily, and she expelled a relieved breath. His mouth curved into the semblance of a smile—that mocked him. 'Not even I can use that excuse twice.'

'Excuse?'

He caressed her cheek gently with the back of his

hand. 'Mmm . . . for my own inability to control my instincts where you're concerned. For not being able to ignore you.'

Mallory's heart constricted. 'You would rather—ignore me?'

'I would!' he said drily.

'Because I'm an employee?'

'Because I don't trust my feelings any more!' Bren's broad chest rose and fell deeply, and he added in a rueful tone, 'Because I didn't want to become involved with you!'

His disclosures filled Mallory with both pleasure and pain. Pleasure, because he had as good as admitted to some emotional involvement with her—and pain, because he seemed to regret its having happened.

'But why not with—me?' she forced herself to ask, if tentatively. She took a deep breath, resolutely disregarding her own reluctance to make comparisons on the subject, and reminded him, 'You were involved with—Charlene.'

'And the only similarity you have to her is that you're also female!' Bren retorted roughly. Shifting, he cupped her face between his hands. 'Charlene was . . .' he shrugged deprecatingly, 'simply convenient and—very willing! To put it bluntly—or callously, if you prefer—she filled a basic need . . . nothing more!' He paused, his mouth tilting crookedly. 'Whereas you, my pet . . .' that tinge of self-mockery began to make a re-appearance in his voice, 'have an effect on me like no other woman I've ever known! You rile me faster, you disturb and disrupt my thoughts more . . . and you arouse emotions only you seem able to fulfil.'

But only of a physical nature? Mallory wondered sadly, noting once again his omission of any deeper feeling. Nonetheless, he had said she affected him like no other woman had, she reminded herself, and for the present she really wasn't in the mood for despondent self-doubts. Not while she was so agreeably aware of his virile masculine length fitted so companionably to hers, his sinewed arms satisfyingly ensuring she remained close, and she felt so contentedly languid.

'Although you're not still annoyed that I came, are you?' she ventured to ask softly.

Bren eyed their familiarly entangled figures expressively. 'At this point of time, that could be somewhat difficult to claim,' he returned on a dry note.

Mallory smiled, but hesitated as she trailed her fingers across his hard chest. 'Does that also mean I can come again?'

His mouth shaped wryly. 'Since I don't recall issuing an invitation this time, would whatever I said make any difference?'

She nodded. 'I didn't know you would be here today.'

'So I gathered from the look on your face when you saw me,' he acknowledged in suddenly weighty tones punctuated by a long exhaled breath. 'What did you think me capable of doing to you?' His brows drew together in a frown.

'Murder!' she quipped, although not altogether tongue-in-cheek. 'I mean, not in my wildest dreams did I imagine you were going to be at all welcoming, and . . . ' she slanted him an eloquent glance, 'you weren't, were you?'

Bren sighed, ironically. 'No—well—I must admit a little slaughter did have a certain appeal at the time. I wasn't expecting you here, I hadn't wanted you here . . . and quite frankly, it didn't help to find that you'd already managed to subvert Lew's loyalties as well!'

'As if I could!' Mallory said with a half-laugh. 'That man would never go against you, Bren Dalton . . . and you know it! He offered me some kind support, that's all.'

'Hmm . . .' He appeared to give the matter some rueful thought as he threaded his fingers idly in the long strands of her hair. 'Support you wouldn't have needed if I hadn't been here. So if you didn't know I was here today, why did you come, Mallory?' A watchful look filtered back into his eyes again.

Seeing it, Mallory despaired of his ever completely losing that mistrust, but she determinedly pretended not to have noticed his change in mood as she answered truthfully, 'I wanted to know why you came here every weekend.'

'*Why* I came here?'

'Mmm.' Her lips curved obliquely. 'It never occurred to me that you might own Kianawah.'

'So what *did* you think brought me here?'

Mallory swallowed and shied away from what had been her most compelling, revealing reason. Instead, she shrugged diffidently and temporised. 'Friends maybe, or I even thought your—father might perhaps live here.' She sent him an apologetic look. 'I didn't know at the time that he was dead.'

'Lew told you, eh?'

Although he drawled it indolently, Mallory still wasn't sure of his mood, so she propped herself up on one elbow to regard him anxiously. 'You won't have words with him about it, will you?'

To her relief, Bren shook his head. 'How can I censure him for having been bewitched by you, when it would appear you've done the same to me?' he countered in a return to his mocking tone.

Thankful to have at least dispelled the suspicion from his eyes, Mallory dared to cast him a mischievously chiding glance from under her lashes. 'Well—if you had been a little more willing to volunteer some information yourself . . .'

Momentarily, Bren moved his head in a wryly resigned gesture, his gaze indulgent, and then his expression sobered. 'I've never been one for discussing either myself or my life, sweetheart,' he said gruffly.

'Except with Lew!' she was quick to qualify. It was an important factor to her. It was vital evidence that his trust *could* be gained!

'Except with Lew,' he granted. 'But then, I've known him for almost twenty years.'

'While I've only known you for two months!' She made an expressive moue. 'Be that as it may, though . . .' she smiled in a teasing, superior fashion now, 'and despite your efforts to the contrary, it still might surprise you to know just how much I've learnt about you simply from my own observations.'

Tucking his arms behind his head, Bren regarded her lazily from beneath lashes that were as thick and curling as hers. 'Such as?'

Mallory began ticking them off on her fingers. 'You're honest—even if not always complimentary; you're hard-working and exceptionally good at what you do—although not to the point of self-importance; you're not devious in your dealings,' she swallowed self-consciously, 'even when you consider others are; and I think you also have a well developed sense of humour—even if sardonically expressed most times. Also, I know from experience that you *can* be kind, and you're also obviously very loyal.' The latter trait gave his mother's infidelity and disloyalty even greater impact, she suspected.

'Yeah—well—you forgot cynical, derogatory, cruel, unfair, sceptical, disparaging, plus a host of similar characteristics . . . all of which you've also accused me of being,' he said ironically.

Because he disagreed, or merely because he was wary of admitting to them, to her at least? Mallory found herself wondering.

'And just how would you know whether I was loyal or not, anyway?' Bren's blue eyes sought hers chafingly.

Undeterred, Mallory returned his gaze squarely. 'Because you gave Lew a home when, as he said himself, he was too old for anyone else to hire him, and . . .' she inclined her head contemplatively, 'because I suspect it could even be loyalty that's keeping you at Banfield's now, when I don't doubt you would rather be putting in all your time on Kianawah.'

'You don't think, with all the capital required to get this place going again, that my salary could be the incentive?' he asked.

'Is it?'

Bren uttered a disbelieving half-laugh. 'Don't you know that's nothing to do with you?' he chided.

'Although . . . *you* raised the subject!' she was quick to retort in turn with a smile.

'Don't remind me!' Bren glanced ceilingwards in despair, and Mallory couldn't decide which of them was the more surprised when he actually relented to concede, 'OK, then the answer is, yes, the money is really all that's keeping me there these days.'

'These days?' She couldn't help but persist. And in response to his suffering look, 'Well, you can't expect to leave it only half explained.'

'Apparently not!' accompanied by another gaze

askance. Stretching lazily, he settled her closer to him, his fingers caressing the satin skin of her shoulder. 'So . . . when I first bought Kianawah there wasn't anyone in Banfield's who could have taken over my position immediately. With that further two years' training, there is someone who could logically do so now, but . . .' he shrugged philosophically, 'this place still needs the injection of that extra capital for another year or two before it really can become self-supporting.'

Mallory nodded thoughtfully. 'I see.' There was a moment's hesitation and then she hazarded, 'This is also where you were planning on coming during your holiday, isn't it?'

Bren looked at her from the corners of his eyes. 'Until someone saw fit to have it postponed,' he acceded in expressive tones.

'I'm sorry.' She bit at her lip contritely. 'I really didn't mean that to happen. I thought J.B. would consider it sufficient for Ward to do the supervising.'

'Yeah—well—what's done is done.' He brushed her apology aside lazily.

Mallory drew a deep breath. 'Although you haven't yet said whether I'm welcome to visit again,' she said tentatively.

Bren quirked a lightly mocking brow. 'You mean, you are actually giving me the choice next time?'

Emboldened by the humour in his tone, she smiled provocatively. 'Do you want one?'

For a moment Bren remained motionless, seemingly mesmerised by her curving mouth, and then he gave an awed shake of his head. 'Dear God, you are just so incredibly beautiful that sometimes I find it hard to believe you're real!' he confessed huskily.

'Oh, I'm real all right. Very real.' Moving even closer to him, Mallory pressed a lingering kiss to his bare, bronzed shoulder. 'Can't you feel?'

'Too much, I'm thinking!' he growled as he shifted lithely to lean over her, and his mouth compulsively sought the warm hollow at the base of her throat.

'So I can come, then?' Mallory whispered unevenly.

Bren's lips scorched a burning path to her rounded breasts. 'What do you think?' he groaned.

'I think . . . I must have been—only half alive before I met you,' she whispered on a ragged breath, and moaned softly when his mouth captured and invaded hers with a slow, devouring hunger.

CHAPTER NINE

MALLORY left Kianawah before Bren the next morning. Of necessity, they had to return by their different forms of transport, but there was still a smile on her lips and a glow in her eyes knowing he would be at Avalon, waiting for her, by the time she arrived. In fact, it made the journey seem much shorter, so that she was pleasantly surprised with the speed with which she reached Avalon later in the day.

On driving up to the homestead, the sight of a red Porsche parked near the house brought her a moment's puzzlement as she wondered who the owner might be, and the reason for their presence. However, on seeing her stepfather emerge on to the veranda, with another man close behind him, she forgot about the Porsche as she hurriedly parked Ward's car in the garage and started across the intervening ground.

Only by now, Mallory realised, it wasn't just two men on the veranda, but four, although that did nothing to dim her smile of pleasure on seeing Bren among them, if somewhat to the rear. The man already descending the steps was nowhere near as retiring, though. He continued towards her swiftly.

'Mallory! At last! We've been waiting for you since just after lunch!' he exclaimed.

'Eric?' she mouthed faintly, astonishment slowing her steps and her reflexes when, on reaching her, he kissed her proprietorially. 'Wh-what on earth are you doing here?'

'Accepting your invitation, of course,' he said, clasping her about the waist. His dark brown eyes ranged over her stunned features broodingly. 'Since you've chosen to bury yourself out here, it became obvious I would have to come to you, if you weren't going to come to me.'

Mallory shook her head in confusion and repudiation. 'But I didn't invite you here!' she gasped.

'Yes, you did,' he insisted, beginning to urge her along with him towards the homestead. 'You can't have forgotten, surely? It was during the Melbourne Cup race-meeting.'

With her wits starting to return, Mallory's first reaction was to look in Bren's direction, and her heart immediately plummeted on finding him surveying the scene with a hard-eyed and tight-lipped gaze before he turned on his heel in a contemptuous movement and disappeared inside. Oh, curse Eric for having come here! she railed fiercely. And . . . curse Bren, too, for even now being so willing to suspect the worst! The addition came brokenly. Although it was the man with her upon whom she vented most of her feelings.

'That particular race-meeting was over three years ago, Eric!' she gritted, pulling free of his hold.

Despite looking a trifle taken aback by her vehemence, he still didn't appear abashed, she noticed. 'But country people have always been known for their hospitality . . . and welcome, no matter when the invitation was made,' he returned blithely.

'Unless circumstances happen to have changed, of course!' she snapped.

'Well, there you are, then.' Eric smiled complacently. Infuriatingly, from Mallory's point of view. 'I don't know why you mentioned it, because certainly nothing's changed in the way I feel about you. And . . .' his voice began to deepen, 'how could your feelings about me have changed either, since you've been stuck out here ever since you returned?'

Mallory wasn't going to tell him. Instead, she merely shrugged and tried to impress on him, 'Except that I never really was looking for a relationship with you, Eric!'

'But that was then, when you had your sights set on going overseas to further your career, and although I was naturally disappointed, I still could understand it,' he assured her earnestly and caught her close again with an arm about her shoulders. 'But there's nothing like that to come between us now! You know how I've always felt about you, Mallory, and I'm sure our just spending some time together will be enough to confirm your feelings for me!'

'Just your being here has already done that, believe me!' she retorted with a sarcastically expressive grimace, but to her despair he was so absorbed with his own thoughts on the matter that he took her words at face value.

'You don't know how happy that makes me,' he murmured in intense tones close to her ear. 'But it will be my pleasure to show you . . . later!' His fingers tightened their grip on her shoulder meaningfully.

Having reached the steps, there was no time for Mallory to reply, only to glance at him aghast, before making her way on to the veranda.

She had already recognised Duncan Amery as not only the man left with her stepfather, but also the owner of the Porsche—remembering it now from when he and Renata had attended Joshua Banfield's party—and Mallory quickly fixed him with a partly fulminating, partly direful gaze as their glances met. Good lord, he, of all people, knew it wasn't Eric

Cummings who interested her, so why had he brought him?

'Duncan. What a *lovely* surprise!' she greeted him with pungent eloquence, and was gratified to see he at least had the grace to look a little shamefaced.

'Mmm, I'm on my way to Adelaide for business. And when Eric discovered I was driving over there . . .' He spread his hands helplessly.

'You thoughtfully brought him with you!' she cooed between tight lips on passing him in order to greet her stepfather.

Ward himself had a pointed aside to make also as he kissed her cheek. 'Well, your trip to—South Australia—didn't take long, did it?'

Mallory caught her lower lip between her teeth. She supposed Bren must have told him where she had been. 'Yes—well—I'm sorry for deceiving you, but . . . I—I'll explain later,' she whispered swiftly, uncomfortably, casting a significant glance towards their visitors. Then uncontrollably, and even more urgently, 'Where has Bren gone, anyway?'

Ward cocked his head to one side. 'By the sound of it, I'd say he's off to check on some of the back paddocks or something similar.'

Picking up the sound of the accelerating motor-bike herself now, Mallory nodded despondently. Apparently she wasn't even going to be given the chance to explain!

'Well, shall we return to the sitting-room for another drink?' suggested Eric brightly, evidently the only one of them who felt he had something to be cheerful about. 'I expect Mallory would like one after her drive.'

Mallory definitely felt in need of something, and nodded resignedly. But once she was seated in the sitting-room, and furnished with a cool drink, questions immediately began to form.

'So how long are the two of you staying? Just overnight?' she asked hopefully, her gaze encompassing both Duncan and Eric.

'Well, I am,' Duncan agreed in a faintly awkward manner. 'Ward was kind enough to suggest I might like to. But as for Eric . . .' He hunched a diffident shoulder.'

'No, I'm staying for the week,' the other man answered for himself. 'After all, your invitation was for a few days, and as I was telling Ward and Bren earlier . . .' He broke off, looking about the room curiously before focusing his attention on Ward. 'Where is Bren? He seems to have disappeared.'

'He left to check on something, I believe,' Ward replied levelly.

'Oh!' Eric's brows rose fractionally, and then he uttered a small, sardonic laugh. 'Perhaps it's just as well, because you couldn't really say he's been pleasant company since we arrived! Heaven knows why, but he seemed to be in as foul a mood as I've ever seen!' He gave a dismissive shake of his head. 'However, to return to what I was saying . . .'

Caught up with her own depressed, and depressing, thoughts, Mallory tuned out of the conversation, and was thankful when her stepfather suggested it was time they prepared for dinner, and she was able to seek the peace and solace of her room. Although, as she restlessly awaited Bren's return, she found neither serenity nor comfort.

She wanted to speak to Bren, make him listen while she explained, and as soon as possible. But as it happened, she had only just entered the shower when she caught the sound of the bike's return, and although she finished washing as quickly as possible and dressed hurriedly afterwards, when she left her room she could still find no sign of him.

'Is Bren in his room?' she asked urgently of Ward on locating her stepfather instead.

He exhaled heavily. 'No, pet, he came in, had a quick shower, and left again a minute ago for town.' His brows lowered. 'Look, I'm not meaning to pry, but just what is . . .'

'*A minute ago*, you said?' Mallory interrupted him anxiously, disregarding everything else and already turning for the door again.

Ward nodded. 'Mmm, that's all. But I do wish you would . . .'

'Later. I'll tell you later,' she broke in on him earnestly, and with a last apologetic, pleading look, went racing down the hallway.

From the veranda, Mallory could see the Range Rover starting to reverse from the garage, and kicking off her hindering high-heeled sandals, she cleared the steps in one bound and flew across the grass on bare feet.

'Bren!' she shouted to attract his attention as the vehicle came to a stop. '*Bren!*' Her voice rose despairingly on seeing the Range Rover beginning to move off, and then she gave a relieved sob when it gradually came to a halt again. 'Aren't you—even going to speak—to me?' Her eyes were shaded with distress and disappointment as they lifted to his on her coming to a panting halt beside the driver's door.

Bren's lips compressed, his expression as remote and hostile as she had ever seen it. 'About what?' he countered coldly, inflexibly, giving a dismissive shrug.

Mallory shook her head in rejection. 'You know very well what about!' She dragged in a deep breath. 'For a start—about . . . Eric.'

His dark brows arched in a gesture of cool disdain. 'And why should I want to speak to you about him? It's your prerogative to invite him here, if that's what you want.' He set the vehicle in motion once more.

Keeping pace with it, she entreated anguishedly, 'But if you would just let me explain!'

Bren muttered something savage under his breath, and applied the brake again—to the Range Rover, at least, if not his temper. 'There's no need!' he grated harshly, his eyes glintig with a steely sheen. 'The look on your face at seeing him, and the way you rushed into his arms, did all the explaining necessary!'

'The way I rushed into *his* arms!' Mallory repeated, dumbfounded, as yet again the four-wheel-drive began to move. '*I was rushing to see . . .*' she started to cry out '. . . you.' The final word fell tremulously from her lips as she gazed desolately after the now fast accelerating vehicle.

Turning showly, she began making her way back to the house with listless steps, and discovered Duncan sitting on the veranda steps eyeing her in a mixture of contrition and compassion.

'Oh, hell, sweetie, what can I say?' he lamented with a sigh. 'Obviously I should never have brought Eric here, should I?'

Mallory shook her head and sank on to the step behind him. 'So why did you, Duncan?' she questioned on a strained note. 'You know he's never really meant anything to me.' She paused. 'But you did know how I felt about Bren!'

He ran a hand around the back of his neck. 'I know, sweetie, but . . . well, I just thought that maybe you'd had a change of heart, or something, when Eric said you'd invited him here.'

'Except that that invitation was issued over three

years ago!' She made an expressive grimace. 'And only then in a spur-of-the-moment fit of bonhomie after a few glasses of champagne because we had just won on a long shot in the Melbourne Cup!'

Duncan ground out an oath. 'The bastard! He led me to believe it was a recent invitation!'

'Yes—well—there's not much that can be done about it now, I guess.' Mallory hunched a regretful shoulder and prepared to rise.

A hand on her arm stayed her. 'But you and—Bren,' Duncan began in tentative tones. 'You actually had—something going?'

Unbidden, the memory of the night before came to torment her, and Mallory closed her eyes quickly to dislodge the picture. 'I think—maybe we could have had,' she owned throatily.

'Oh, I am sorry!' Duncan shook his head in contrition. 'Is there some way I can make amends?'

She shook her head regretfully. 'No, I'm just going to have to impress on Eric that his presence is unwanted and unappreciated, I suppose, and then . . .'

'Concentrate your efforts on setting things right with Bren, hmm?' he broke in, putting his arm around her encouragingly.

Mallory licked at her lips. 'Something like that,' she conceded, in a small voice, as of one accord they began rising to their feet. She was still aware that her only attempt so far to offer an explanation hadn't met with much success!

Perhaps not surprisingly, Mallory found little enjoyment in the evening either. It began badly with the meal Janet had prepared. Fish had never been one of Mallory's favourite foods, no matter how beautifully cooked, and this time was no exception. Consequently, she ate little and drank too much.

None the less, the wine she consumed did at least provide a cushioning barrier, a slight relaxing of tension, that enabled her to get through the evening without either being wholly uncivil to Eric when he showed signs of trying to monopolise her company, or simply bursting into tears at the thought of the havoc he had so carelessly wrought in her life.

Not that her efforts to keep Eric at a distance appeared to deter him at all, Mallory noted. In fact, they merely appeared to increase the intensity of his manner, so that in the end she started to wonder in some alarm if he simply considered she was playing hard to get! It was such an appalling idea that when Duncan, with the excuse that he wanted to be away first thing in the morning, brought the evening to a reasonably early close, Mallory hastily took the opportunity to set about disabusing Eric of the belief that his attentions, or he himself, were welcome.

'I knew you were as anxious for us to be alone as I was,' he declared in a deep tone in response to her advice that she wanted a word with him in private. Draping an arm about her shoulders, he urged her towards the darkened front veranda. 'I've been waiting for this moment all evening.'

Edging out from beneath his arm determinedly, Mallory replied bluntly, I haven't!'

'You haven't?' Eric asked disbelievingly, sinking into a wicker armchair.

Mallory's eyes strayed involuntarily to the track leading to the road as she wondered, for the umpteenth time, when Bren might be likely to return. Then, turning, she gazed down at Eric vexedly. 'Look, I'm not sure why you should suddenly take it into your head to believe I would want to . . .'

'Suddenly!' he interposed thickly, catching hold of
her hand and drawing her closer. 'You know I've felt
this way about you for years! And I said this afternoon
that I would show you, and I will!' He gave an abrupt
tug on her arm that, with the wine already making her
feel less than steady, had her losing her balance and
toppling into his lap.

'Eric!' she protested, struggling ineffectively to
disentangle herself from the arms that were closing
around her. Why hadn't she had less to drink! 'Will
you please . . .'

'Oh, Mallory, I've been wanting to do this all
evening!' he continued in the same fervent accents as if
she hadn't spoken, and before she knew it he was
kissing her hungrily.

Startled, and with her brain reacting fuzzily,
Mallory was momentarily struck motionless—and in
those few brief seconds she heard a heavy tread on the
steps.

'Don't let me interrupt you! I'm just on my way
inside!' Bren said in an acidly cutting voice that
suddenly snapped Mallory into movement, and had
her wrenching free from Eric and scrambling
somewhat inelegantly to her feet.

'Bren!' She put out a hand to catch at his arm, then
withdrew it again, biting at her lip and flushing hotly
as she connected with his raking, derisive gaze.

'Goodnight!' There was a stony note of finality in
his tone, and with a sharp nod of his head that
included them both, he disappeared through the
doorway.

Mallory stared after him, near to tears. He must
have already returned, and been garaging the Range
Rover, when they first came out on to the veranda, she
realised. Oh, if only she had known!

Behind her, Eric reached out to run his fingers up and down her arm. 'Come on, Mallory, there's no call to keep standing there. He won't be back to disturb us again, so let's return to more pleasant pursuits,' he cajoled.

Controlling her emotions with difficulty, Mallory whipped her arm away from his touch and rounded on him balefully. 'I intend to, Eric! Very shortly I shall be going to bed!' she snapped.

'Wh-why, what's wrong?' he stammered in amazement. 'Don't you understand, I want to marry you, Mallory! And I wouldn't make you work like you have to here!' Gaining his feet swiftly, he grasped her by the shoulders. 'With me you would have a life of ease, as someone like you should have! I'd put you on a pedestal, see that you wanted for nothing, ensure you would never have to lift a finger again to anything that even resembled work!'

Mallory shook his hand away impatiently. 'And you're missing the point, Eric! For a start, I don't want to be put on any pedestal!' And certainly not by him, which would mean being classified solely as a decoration in order to reflect *his* achievements! 'What's more, I happen to thoroughly enjoy my work here . . . *and* I have no intention of abandoning it!'

His nostrils flared. 'Why? Because you're hoping to impress *him*?' he sneered, nodding curtly in the direction of the doorway Bren had so recently passed through. 'Do you think I didn't see the look you gave him?'

Mallory returned his gaze challengingly. 'And if I did, it's nobody's business but mine! Although that has nothing to do with my working here!'

'No?' Eric lifted a sardonic brow. 'Well, I can tell you, you're still wasting your time where Bren

Dalton's concerned! For heaven's sake . . .' his tone moderated, became more resonant again, 'even you must have realised by now that he's not looking for any lasting commitments! He never has! Bren doesn't become involved . . . he merely indulges himself!'

'You mean, in the same way you did by suddenly taking up a three-year-old invitation to visit Avalon?' she gibed, refusing to dwell on the more painful aspects of his claims.

'That was different!' he cried. 'I want to marry you. And you know very well that you and I are right for each other, that we've always had—well, an understanding . . .'

'We certainly have never had anything of the kind!' Mallory's furious denial cut his words short. 'Nor have I ever given you reason to believe we had! In fact, the best I can say is that you appear to have confused simple civility for something else entirely!'

'Simple civility?' he scoffed. 'The way you rushed to greet me this afternoon? The way you fell into my arms so willingly only a few minutes ago?'

'Except that it wasn't *you* I was hurrying to greet, and the only reason I fell into your arms was I'd had too much to drink!' she told him baldly.

'You expect me to believe . . .'

'Yes!' she shouted. 'Because for your information, Eric, not only have I never seen you in a romantic light, but I've never even really considered you a friend either! As far as I was concerned, you were always merely an acquaintance . . . and mostly a bloody tiresome one at that!' She was too tired, too annoyed, her emotions too raw, for her to mince her words. 'And now, if you don't mind, I am going to bed—as I said!' She made for the doorway immediately.

'But—but I intended to stay here for a week!' Eric

stammered behind her.

Halting, Mallory expelled an exasperated breath ad threw him a glance over her shoulder. 'In case you haven't guessed . . . your invitation has just been cancelled, Eric!' she enunciated resolutely, and strode on in.

Once inside the homestead, however, other more pressing thoughts came crowding back into Mallory's mind, and for a moment she came to a stop outside Bren's door. Then, with a despondent shake of her head, she continued on to her room. It was probably better left till morning, she decided. When she wouldn't be so tired, nor her brain quite so sluggish . . . and Bren might have become a little more approachable!

As a result of having had somewhat less than her full quota of sleep during the night, coupled with a long drive home, and all the problems that had arisen on her arrival, Mallory didn't wake until far later than usual the following morning.

In consequence, Duncan and Eric were on the point of leaving by the time she emerged from her room. Duncan apparently had offered to drive Eric to the Nyandra airstrip in order either to get a lift with someone who happened to be flying to Melbourne that morning, or else charter a plane to take him there. No sooner had they departed, though, and Mallory and her stepfather had returned inside, than she anxiously sought out Bren's whereabouts.

'I'm sorry, pet, but he left at first light,' Ward told her in weighty tones. He paused, then added even more heavily, 'And I don't think he'll be back for a while either.'

Mallory's heart plunged. 'You're saying—he's left

the property altogether?'

He nodded.

'And did he say where he was going?' To Kianawah, perhaps?

Her stepfather ran a hand through his hair, his gaze troubled as it rested on her strained features. 'No,' he said with a sigh. 'He merely said he would let head office know where he could be contacted.'

'I see.' Mallory pressed her lips together to stop their betraying trembling. 'Well, it would appear we have Avalon to ourselves again, just as in the old days.' She valiantly tried to overcome the anguish that was gnawing at her insides by making light of the matter.

Ward regarded her thoughtfully. 'Except that I suspect something—or someone—else means even more to you than that these days,' he said in a quiet voice.

Mallory bent her head protectively, but decided against a denial. Her stepfather was too astute for that. 'You mean, it actually sh-shows?' she attempted to quip instead, but her voice cracked, and with it her veneer of composure. She burst into ungovernable tears and sobbed out the whole desolating tale.

For a time Mallory felt better for having confided in him, but as each succeeding day passed without so much as a word from Bren, she found some of her emotions undergoing a change. Not those relating to her love for him—those would never alter, she knew without a doubt—nor those causing the despair she was experiencing at his absence, but gradually those of pride and self-respect began to make themselves more strongly felt.

It was they that prevented her from ringing Lew to discover if Bren was indeed at Kianawah, and from getting in touch with Banfield's head office to locate him. They that brought her to the determination that, since he had refused to allow her to explain, it would have to be he who made the next move if their relationship were to proceed. Twice now, she had tried to show how much she cared, but she couldn't—wouldn't—submit to a purely physical liaison again. For her, it wasn't enough. Not when she loved him so much, while he, as Eric had put it, merely indulged himself!

CHAPTER TEN

FORTUNATELY for Mallory, the week following Bren's departure was a busy one, and this helped in some way to keep her mind on matters other than him. She made certain Sunday was no different, even though Ward had gone into Nyandra to visit Cecily, and Dick and Janet, as well as Max Salter, their other station-hand, had also departed for the day.

The morning dawned bright and brassy, an indication of the heat that was to follow, and it reminded her that they were approaching that part of the Victorian summer when bushfires could occur at any time. The lush, tall growth of spring was now tinder dry, just waiting to be ignited—either spontaneously or negligently—and, when fanned by stifling hot winds, this could set off a whirling, searing, uncontrollable blaze that would ravage and blacken anything and everything in its destructive path; incinerating thousands of acres in an afternoon.

Shortly after breakfast, Mallory hitched up the slasher to the tractor and made her way out to one of the back paddocks to begin cutting firebreaks along the fence lines and around areas of heavy tree growth. By lunch time she was hot, thirsty, and sticky. It hadn't seemed to matter in which direction she had driven the tractor, the canopy provided no escape from the sun's relentless pursuit, so she came to a halt alongside a tree-lined creek, grateful for some shade in which to sit while she ate the light meal she had brought with her.

Although the creek was now very shallow, it did possess a much deeper, sandy waterhole that she remembered had been a favourite on hot summer days in the past, and it was to this that she made first. Stripping off her shorts, shirt and sandals, she checked quickly for any new snags that might have been washed into it, and then plunged into the deepest part with a sigh of bliss. The water was neither too warm nor too cold, just refreshingly cool, and she revelled in the feel of it swirling about her heated skin and over her head as she ducked beneath the surface. On emerging again, she turned to wring the excess water from her thick plait, and came to a shocked halt on seeing a man's figure—Bren's figure—on the bank.

'That looks the best place to be on a day like this. Mind if I join you?' he asked quietly.

So unexpected was his appearance—and his actually deigning to speak to her—that Mallory could only shrug as she struggled to find her voice. 'It—it's not my private property,' she pushed out at length. Then more quickly, 'And I was about to get out, anyway.'

In the act of unfastening his shirt, Bren stopped, his blue gaze narrowing as it locked with hers. 'That's not the impression I received.'

Mallory shifted restlessly from one foot to the other. Oh, why did she let him have such an effect on her that, even now, just the sight of him was sufficient to make her heart pound? 'I—well—I wouldn't want to be accused of loafing on the job,' she faltered.

'Did I suggest you were?' he countered tautly, divesting himself of his stock boots and socks.

'N-o . . .' She looked away. 'But there's a lot of slashing still to be done.'

'It can wait!' came the peremptory reply. 'You haven't had your lunch yet, in any event.'

'How do you know?' Surprise had her turning back again, and she found he was already approaching the water. Clad only in a pair of dark blue briefs, his skin sleek and darkly tanned, his muscles impressively defined and rippling with strength at every movement, he was so totally male, his physical presence so vital, that she was immediately aware of an uncontrollable stirring within her.

'I checked in the cooler as I passed the tractor,' Bren said carelessly as he reached the water's edge.

Mallory bent her head, desperately trying to forget the feel of his hard and powerful body pressed close to hers. 'Well, I think I'll go and eat it now, then.' She jumped at the excuse offered, and began edging past him as he waded into the water.

'And I think not!' A muscular arm wrapped about her midriff, bearing her backwards quickly into deeper water and then under it as Bren dived.

Mallory came up fighting—both him, and her body's traitorous response. 'You get your hands off me, Bren Dalton!' she stormed, striking out at him wildly. 'I'll leave this pool when *I* want to, do you hear! You refuse even to speak to me; you disappear for a week without a word; and now you think you can just turn up again when you feel like it and start behaving as if you have rights where I'm concerned! Well, you haven't! Or didn't it occur to you that maybe this time I might not be willing to speak to *you*?' A sarcastic nuance surfaced as she swung an arm towards him yet again.

Evading it by simply releasing her and stepping back, Bren further unsettled her by owning heavily, 'Yes, it occurred to me.' His eyes narrowed. 'But . . . because of Eric?'

'Eric!' she shouted. 'You think I need him as an excuse? How you do underrate yourself! But then, why ask me, anyway? After all, you much prefer to make your own deductions!' Her breasts rose and fell sharply. 'And to hell with whether they're right or wrong, or the effect they may have on anyone else!'

'Meaning?'

Mallory affected an off-hand shrug and began moving to shallower water. 'I'll leave you to come to your own conclusions,' she declared glibly. 'As I said, you're good at that! And judging by past experience, you doubtless will, no matter what I say.' Her gaze turned bitter.

Bren scrubbed a hand through his wet hair roughly. 'OK, so perhaps I am too suspicious,' he granted unexpectedly. 'I apologise! Is that what you wanted to hear?'

'A week ago, maybe!'

'And now?' His eyes never left hers as he started to move slowly towards her.

Mallory licked nervously at her lips and began backing away. 'Now it doesn't matter any more,' she claimed defensively, although not entirely steadily.

'Doesn't it? Then why are you so on edge that you need to keep such a distance between us, hmm? Could this have something to do with it perhaps?' Without warning, Bren covered the space separating them, catching her easily before she could flee further than the water's edge and spinning her back into his imprisoning arms.

'No!' Mallory had time only to dissent before his mouth closed resolutely over hers, with the skill she both yearned for and fought against. Then her struggles became more frantic as she felt him lower them both to the sand, and she tried desperately to twist away from the maddening, enflaming feel of his hard, slickly wet body as it slid over hers. 'No, I won't

let you do this to me, Bren! I won't!' she half-panted,
half-sobbed, at last managing to drag her lips free from
the disruptive contact with his.

Bren's tongue stroked her earlobe and she trembled
helplessly. 'Then what is it you *do* want, Mallory?' he
murmured in a voice that was surprisingly uneven.

What did she want? She wanted to spend the rest of
her life with him, to bear his children, to grow old with
him! With an anguished shudder, she turned her face
away. 'Everything you *don't* want!' she choked.

His fingers caressed the exposed length of her fragile
jaw. 'I want you,' he said softly, and her head snapped
back to his again.

'Only until the next time you feel inclined to distrust
me, of course!' she charged in gibing tones.

Bren shook his head slowly. 'Permanently.'

Mallory's heart missed a beat. 'You mean . . . in a
live-in arrangement?' Her even white teeth caught at
her lower lip doubtfully.

'Uh-uh!' Hesitating, he cupped her face between
the palms of his hands, and then added on a deepening
note, 'I mean . . . I came back here today because I
couldn't stay away from you any longer, because I
could only hope that my scepticism hadn't already
killed what we had together, and because . . . I want
you as my wife!'

Unable to bring herself to believe it, despite her
pulse racing, Mallory's eyes lifted to his uncertainly.
'You really mean that?' She sought reassurance in a
throaty whisper.

Bren released a long breath, his mouth gradually
assuming a wry cast. 'Since I never expected to hear
myself say that to any woman, you'd better believe I
meant it when I did say it,' he recommended.

'Oh, Bren!' With no necessity to conceal her feelings any more, Mallory wound her arms tightly about his neck. 'I love you so much! When you wouldn't let me explain about Eric last week . . .'

His descending mouth cut off her words effectively and satisfyingly. 'I know, sweetheart, and I'm sorry,' he murmured at length. Then, exhaling ruefully, he reversed their positions so that she was lying on top of him. 'But when he arrived, spouting about how he'd been invited because the two of you were on such close terms, and then you seemed so pleased to see him . . .'

'Oh, you deserve to be hit for that, Bren Dalton!' she interrupted, and in fact she grabbed hold of two handfuls of his hair mock-threateningly. 'It was you I was delighted at the thought of seeing again! How could you have possibly thought Eric might mean anything to me after the night I had just spent with you?'

Bren flexed an excusing shoulder. 'Well, you didn't offer much resistance when he kissed you.'

'Because I was so stunned that he should even have done so!'

'And on the veranda later?' He crooked an explicit brow.

Mallory flushed at the memory, and then rallied. 'Well, that was all your fault, as it happens,' she chided. 'Because if you hadn't upset me so much, I wouldn't have drunk so much during the evening, with the result that when Eric became amorous I wouldn't have overbalanced on to his lap and had to suffer his unpleasant, and definitely unwanted, kissing.'

His lips twitched. 'Is that what happened?'

She nodded. 'And I'll have you know that immediately thereafter I cancelled his three-year-old invitation to visit—which had only been impulsively issued in the first place—and he left the same morning you did! Only he did at least wait around long enough to say goodbye!' She fixed him with a meaningful glance.

Bren lifted a hand to toy idly with her plait as it rested on her shoulder, his expression sobering. 'I couldn't stand the thought of seeing you with him again. I had just discovered you meant more to me than anything else in my life, and . . . well, when you obviously could have your pick from so many, I couldn't bring myself to believe you could really want me. I've so little to offer you; nowhere near what Eric could . . .'

'Maybe not, possession-wise, but it was someone very special I fell in love with,' she inserted fervently. 'Besides, I as good as told you at J.B.'s party that Eric held no interest for me.'

'Mmm, as I recall, you implied someone else had already caught your eye,' ironically.

Mallory bent her head to brush her lips tantalisingly over his muscular chest. 'And will always continue to do so,' she averred in expressive tones.

Bren gazed at her wonderingly, his blue eyes dark with feeling. 'God, how I love you!' he groaned thickly, and set his mouth to the warmly beating hollow of her throat. 'You storm into a man's life, his heart, his soul even, until you become his very reason for existing!' He shook his head. 'I guess I should have known what was happening when it kept irritating me so much that night to see you with other men! It seems even then my thoughts were beginning to linger too often and for too long on you!'

Mallory drew back a space. 'You're regretting it?' she teased, straight-faced.

His arms tightened about her possessively, the expression on his face making her breath catch in her throat. 'When I want you—will always want you—with every fibre of my being? Never!' He paused, the cast of his features changing slightly as he sighed. 'Although that, unfortunately, doesn't alter the fact that while I have to continue working for Banfield's, we won't be able to see as much of one another as we might like, even after we're married.' His mouth sloped regretfully. 'So would you prefer to remain at Avalon, or . . .'

'I intend only to be wherever my husband is,' she said determinedly. There was a slight pause. 'And that's at Kianawah!'

Bren made a deprecatory gesture. 'As much as the idea appeals, love, I'm afraid it's just not possible at present.'

Mallory returned his gaze resolutely. 'But I have something to contribute to our lives together, too!' She tilted her head quizzically, a bantering light twinkling in her amethyst eyes. 'Or would my offering some—er—financial assistance, constitute a blow to your male pride?'

He hunched a tanned shoulder. 'If it benefits you, I guess not,' he allowed wryly. 'So how much are you wishing to—contribute?'

'Well, I'm not sure of the exact amount at the moment, but . . .' she dimpled engagingly, 'how does half a million sound?'

For a moment Bren neither spoke nor moved. He simply stared at her, incredulously. Then he shook his head sharply, as if to clear it, and half demanded, half laughed, 'Are you serious?'

An impish grin caught at Mallory's lips. 'Trading on one's face and figure—as someone once put it,' she inserted with a feigned look of severity, 'can be extremely rewarding financially if one is fortunate enough to have the look that's in favour at the time,' she said. 'And I did tell you I'd had aspirations to purchase Avalon myself, if possible.' She shrugged. 'Well, when that fell through due to Banfield's buying it first, I didn't waste what I'd already saved, I simply added to it and invested it—in case something else came along. And now it has.' She laughed delightedly.

Bren uttered something expressive beneath his breath. 'But it never occurred to me you would have . . .' He shook his head. 'Do you realise what you've just made possible?'

Mallory nodded happily. 'Mmm, I've helped us both achieve what we wanted. You, to devote all your time and effort to upgrading Kianawah, and me, to be always with the man I love instead of having your work continually separating us every time you're required in Melbourne, or Queensland, or South Australia, etcetera.'

'Dear God, I adore you!' he vowed, and kissed her lingeringly. 'I wasn't sure just how I was going to manage to endure those separations. These last few days certainly taught me that life wasn't worth living without you!' Pausing, he eyed her tenderly. 'At the same time, though . . . will you mind too much leaving Avalon? I know how you feel about the place.'

Mallory's expression turned thoughtful. 'It will be hard, I admit. It holds so many happy memories,' she owned slowly. 'However . . .' she continued in a lighter tone, 'with you there, I'm very sure Kianawah will soon come to replace it adequately.'

Bren's arms tightened about her implicitly. 'Well, at least you've proved me right in one thing,' he declared. A wide, taunting, and totally heart-shaking smile made an appearance. 'I always said you'd never see it through as manager here.'

With a laugh, Mallory reciprocated with a

deliberately provocative glance from beneath her long lashes. 'Well—if you would rather I did remain . . .'

'Only right where you are!' he retorted in a growling voice, and then shook his head. 'I used to believe that love, caring, made you weak and vulnerable, but with you—especially here, like this—I know I've never felt more sure or happier in my life!'

'And I intend to make certain you never feel otherwise,' she promised softly, and he urged her head down to his, his lips meeting hers in a long, drugging kiss that had her senses reeling.

'Oh, I want you!' Bren groaned on a huskily deep note, his hands caressing the silken skin of her back. Unfastening the clip of her bra, he slid the straps from her shoulders and Mallory helped him dispose of it completely, luxuriating in the stimulating feel of his firm flesh pressing against the yielding softness of her own.

'Here . . .?' She smiled and spared a moment to look about them expressively.

Bren eased her on to her back, his mouth already beginning to seek hers again. 'Could anywhere be more appropriate?' he asked, his fingers moving to the curve of her hip, and Mallory was inclined to agree with him.

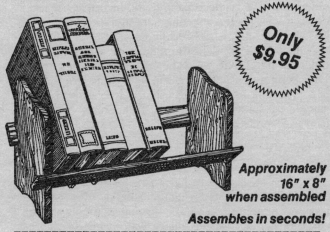

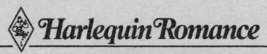 **Harlequin Romance**

Coming Next Month

2953 BLIND TO LOVE Rebecca Winters
When Libby Anson joins her husband in Kenya, she's shocked by his announcement that their marriage is over. He insists that his blindness changes everything. But it doesn't—not for Libby.

2954 FETTERS OF GOLD Jane Donnelly
Nic is in love with Dinah. Although Dinah isn't as sure of her feelings for Nick, there's no way she'll let his overbearing cousin Marcus dictate what they can or cannot do!

2955 UNEXPECTED INHERITANCE Margaret Mayo
Alice is far from delighted at the prospect of a visit to the West Indies, all expenses paid. It means giving in to the commands of her unknown grandfather's will. Worse still, it means seeing Jared Duvall again....

2956 WHEN TWO PATHS MEET Betty Neels
Katherine is properly grateful to Dr. Jason Fitzroy for rescuing her from the drudgery of her brother's household and helping her to find a new life-style. She can't help dreaming about him, though she's sure he's just being kind.

2957 THE CINDERELLA TRAP Kate Walker
Dynamic Matt Highland doesn't connect the stunning model Clea with the plump unattractive teenager he'd snubbed years ago. But Clea hasn't forgotten—or forgiven—and she devises a plan to get even!

2958 DEVIL MOON Margaret Way
Career girl Sara is a survivor in the jungle of the television world, but survival in the real jungle is a different matter, as she finds out when her plane crashes. There, she is dependent on masterful Guy Trenton to lead the party to safety....

Available in January wherever paperback books are sold, or through Harlequin Reader Service:

In the U.S.
901 Fuhrmann Blvd.
P.O. Box 1397
Buffalo, N.Y. 14240-1397

In Canada
P.O. Box 603
Fort Erie, Ontario
L2A 5X3

Harlequin Historicals

Step into a world of pulsing adventure, gripping
emotion and lush sensuality with these evocative
love stories penned by today's best-selling authors
in the highest romantic tradition. Pursuing their
passionate dreams against a backdrop of the past's
most colorful and dramatic moments, our vibrant
heroines and dashing heroes will make history
come alive for you.

Watch for two new Harlequin Historicals each
month, available wherever Harlequin books are
sold. History was never so much fun—you won't
want to miss a single moment!

GHIST-1